Choose Your
TANGLED WEB OF FATE

A *Tangled Web of Friends* story

Valerie Lofaso

Runestone Publishing
Portsmouth, New Hampshire, USA

ISBN TBD

Cataloging in Publication Data
TBD

Library of Congress Control Number: TBD

Editing by Charles Richard, Lin Richard, and Nomar Slevik

Book design by Runestone Publishing

Printed in the United States of America

Runestone Publishing
120 Ledgewood Dr. #10
Portsmouth, NH 03801

First Edition

This book is dedicated to my pre-teen self who was obsessed
with the gamebook-style books.

For my cousin Cathi, who taught me how to read through all the
different storylines.

And as always, for Juliana. Always follow your heart!

Welcome! You are about to embark on a different type of literary journey. This book doesn't work like other books. You will start on page 1 and then read until you reach one of three things:
-    A single directive
-    A choice of two directives
-    THE END

A directive will send you to another page. A choice will offer you two different directions to go. You must choose one, and then go to that page. If you reach a point that says 'THE END' then that is where that story line ends. You must go back to the beginning and try again. There are many different ways to go in this story. Some are good, some are fun, some are tragic. But the choice is always yours.

Turn now to page 1. Good luck and happy ghost hunting!

You are the new kid in school. You have only been there for two weeks, but you made friends with two girls named Josie York and Jenna LaPage, along with Jenna's brother Simon LaPage and her boyfriend Dave Miller. You quickly find out that they are paranormal investigators, and now they have invited you on an investigation with them this Saturday. You are not entirely sure you want to go – though you don't really believe in ghosts, the idea that they *might* exist scares you – but you don't want to let down your new friends. You reluctantly agree to go.

Late Saturday afternoon you arrive at Jenna's house. Josie and Dave are already there. Dave is tall and muscular, and you remember hearing at school that he is one of the star athletes. You feel better about this investigation knowing a big, tough guy like him will be there. *If he can handle it, so can I*, you tell yourself.

Jenna is sitting on the floor of her bedroom, surrounded by electronic equipment of all kinds. She looks up and smiles at you when you walk in the room. "Hi! Glad you could make it! It's going to be great to have a fourth member of our team. My brother Simon used to be the fourth, but he doesn't like this ghost stuff much, so he's out and you're in!"

You just smile at her, trying to show enthusiasm instead of nervousness, and sit on the floor with her.

"Okay, so this is my equipment. I figure, the more equipment we use, the more evidence we'll get. And if we can get multiple pieces of evidence to back each other up, then we just might have actual proof!" Jenna says. "Now, I want to tell you a little about the equipment and how we use it. These are digital video cameras that can shoot in regular mode or night vision. We use it mostly in night vision mode. This is a regular still digital camera. We try to take pictures with a standard digital camera of everything for our records – pictures of the inside and outside of the location, pictures of places where paranormal activity is most reported, like things moving, apparitions, and that kind of thing. This is a K-2 meter for detecting electromagnetic energy, these are audio recorders for capturing EVPs, and these are flashlights that we use not only to see in the dark, of course, but we sometimes use them to try to communicate with spirits. Oh, and of course there's our most important piece of equipment, Josie!"

You look at Jenna, overwhelmed and confused. Jenna chuckles. Josie rolls her eyes and sighs. "What she means is that I am a Medium. That's right. I talk to dead people. And Jenna uses that to her advantage."

"Okay, I think you two have overwhelmed our new friend here," says Dave. "Maybe you should take it easy."

"Sorry," Jenna says to you. "I know this is a lot to take in. Why don't I just tell you about the place we're investigating?"

"Sure," you say.

"Okay, Josie, you know what that means," says Jenna.

"Yup," says Josie. "I'll go pack up our snacks."

When Josie has closed the door behind her, Jenna answers the question you were about to ask. "Because she's a Medium, I don't want her to know anything about the investigation beforehand. That way, anything she picks up on we know is not something she already knew. It helps us validate evidence. Does that make sense?"

You nod.

"Okay, so my wonderful boyfriend Dave is the one who got us this investigation. His mom has a friend who is a realtor. She just purchased a big old factory building that's been empty for years. She brought in a construction crew to fix it up a bit, just clean it up, fix some broken windows, make sure everything is structurally sound. Well, the foreman on the job quit the other day, taking his whole crew with him, and leaving the job half done. At first, he refused to say why, but Donna, the realtor, threatened him with a lawsuit for breach of contract. That was when he broke down in tears and confessed. His crew had been complaining over the two weeks they had worked that things would go missing: tools, lunch boxes, coffee cups, cell phones. The guy didn't think much of it until they started to say they were seeing things – shadows moving along the hallways, arms or legs disappearing through doorways. He thought it was people, like real, live people, because they'd had problems with homeless people and teenagers breaking into the building over the years. So, after his guys complained over and over, he decided to take a look around the building to see if he could find where they were getting in. He was in the basement, and he saw a guy down there. He yelled at him 'Hey! You can't be in here!' The guy turned, looked at him, and disappeared before his eyes!"

"Wow!" you say. A shiver runs up your spine.

"I know, right? A full-bodied apparition that looked like a man but disappeared! This is the best case ever!" said Jenna. She then looks at you. "So, are you ready for this?"

If you want to chicken out, go to page 12
If you want to continue, go to page 24

"I'll stay with Josie and Simon, if that's okay with you," you reply.

"Fine by me," Jenna and Josie both say.

"I want to set up a camera while we're down here," Jenna says, and sets to work quickly putting a camera on a tripod near the stairs, aiming into the vast darkness of basement. "Okay, see you guys in a bit," she says when done, and she and Dave start up the stairs.

"So, what's next?" you ask Josie.

"I have some more energy to feel out down here, and then we can head upstairs again," she replies.

You look at Simon. "Did you want to take over the walk-through?" you ask, holding out the camera for him.

He shakes his head. "Not unless you want me to."

"I'm enjoying it," you say. "And I think I'm doing an okay job." You look at Josie.

"You're doing a great job," she says. She starts to walk toward the back of the basement. "Things have calmed down a little bit since I did the salt circle, so that's good. But there are still so many lost souls here." She goes on to describe a very unhappy man whose body had been dumped in the swamp after he was killed for not giving in to blackmail by his boss. Then she describes a young woman who died in a car accident on the street outside and was thrown from the car. In her confusion, she took shelter in the old building and has been chased around by various nefarious ghosts ever since. Josie continues describing various other ghosts and residual impressions as she walks through the basement then makes her way up to the first floor.

Josie is partway down the hall when she stops and says, "Sam just introduced me to a father and son, Edward and Eddie. They're talking to me, but they have no idea they're dead. Sam says that he's tried to make them understand but they either can't, or they just refuse to believe it."

"Do you know how they died?" you ask.

"Sam says that the father died here during construction. A wall collapsed on him and crushed him. The son then came to work here after it was finished and died exactly five years to the day his father died when he tried to break up a fight between two other workers, got shoved, and he fell down the stairs," says Josie.

"Wow," you say with a frown.

"I have an idea," Simon says then. "Josie, can you tell me where the father and son are standing?"

"Sure. The son, Eddie, is in front of you about three feet and his father is standing a little to his left, your right."

"Okay," Simon says, then looks at the air where Edward is standing. You follow with the camera. "Hey, Edward. If you and your son aren't dead, could I do this?"

Simon takes three rapid, long strides forward. Josie gasps, and you understand what Simon just did.

"Josie, can you tell us what you see?" you ask.

Josie nods. "They are both… in shock, I think. Edward looks a little mad. Eddie is still confused. No, wait… I think Eddie's understanding what just happened and why. He's fading into a golden mist. He's gone! Wow…. Oh, but Edward's definitely angry."

"I get that you're angry, Edward," Simon says, seemingly talking to the air. "I made your son disappear. Because he's dead. Because you're dead, too. Don't you get that?"

"Simon, that's not very compassionate," Josie says.

"Ouch," he says, but not to Josie. He grabs his back and doubles over.

"Yeah, Edward just punched you in the kidneys," Josie scoffs.

"I didn't deserve that!" Simon says.

"Okay, okay… Edward, I apologize that my friend here did what he did," Josie says. "He may have acted a bit hastily, but if you think about it, the end result is what is best for your son. It's what is best for you, too."

Josie falls silent for a few minutes. Simon is able to stand straight but he continues to rub his lower back. Then Josie continues, "I understand that you're afraid of what's out there, but being here, stuck in this building, and now you're without your son…. I think you're wrong, that he was naïve to go. I think once he realized he is dead, he felt the tug to the other side, and he felt the goodness that comes from it. I've had other people like him and like you tell me about it. You should try to let yourself feel it just a little bit."

She pauses again, and after a few beats, turns to you and Simon and says, "He's being stubborn. He's scared."

"Why can't Sam help?" you ask.

"Sam is scared, too. Most of them are. They know they did something bad in life, so they are afraid of what might happen to them when they move on," Josie says.

"You mean, Hell, right?" you ask.

Josie nods.

"Isn't that a valid, logical fear?" you ask.

"Logical, yes, but I don't know if it's valid," she says.

"What do you mean?" you ask.

"Well, I don't really have time to go into it, but based on all the ghosts I have helped, I'm not sure Hell exists. And eventually I will need to convince Edward of that to help him cross over, but I guess for now we should finish the walk-through. Okay?" Josie looks at you and Simon.

"Okay, lead the way," you say. Josie continues on down the hall.

Behind you, Simon says, "Have you heard the term 'down the rabbit hole'?"

"Yeah," you reply.

"Well, this is one of those rabbit holes that once you get inside you realize that there are hundreds of more holes to explore," he says.

"The best thing to do is keep a mental list of all your questions and ask them later," Josie says, over her shoulder.

"Okay," you say. Once again, you feel a bit overwhelmed.

Josie reaches the end of the hall where the equipment room is, peeks inside, but turns around and starts back down the hall.

"Is anything happening that you should tell the camera?" you ask after several moments of silence.

"We're going up to the third floor," she says quickly over her shoulder.

To go to the third floor, go to page 31

"The break room sounds intriguing to me," you say.

"I agree," says Simon.

"Alright, let me get you guys set up with equipment and then you can head on up," Jenna says. "We all wear audio recorders that run at all times. That way when the investigation is over, we can sync the recorders and video to help us know where everyone was during the night and who made what sounds. It helps eliminate false evidence of EVPs and shadows and things. It also increases our chances of capturing an EVP since, theoretically, they can happen at any time." Then, she gives Simon a video camera, hands you a walkie talkie, and gives you both flashlights.

"Okay, stairs are at the end of this hall. Go to the second floor, through the big room, down the hall, last door on the right," Jenna says, and you nod.

"After you," Simon says to you, gesturing for you to go through the doorway first. You hesitate for only a moment – you already feel like a fool for bailing on your friends earlier, and you want to show them you are not a chicken – so you charge through the doorway into the dark hall. There are rooms on both sides of the hallway so only small specks of light from outside can be seen through the dirty windows of the rooms as you pass by. Your flashlight only breaks the darkness for a few feet ahead at a time which hardly seems like enough when you have no idea where you are going. As you walk, you search the darkness around you for movement and strain your ears for sounds other than the sounds of your and Simon's feet on the dirty cement floor. You do your best to keep your breathing steady as fear creeps in on you, and then suddenly you are at the stairs to the upper level.

There is a gaping hole in the floor to the right for the stairwell to the basement that oozes a sense of foreboding. You shiver.

"You okay?" Simon asks, his voice echoing a little.

"Yes, fine," you say, and start up the stairs.

You reach the second floor. Stairs continue on up to the next level and in front of you is a double set of doors. One is open while the other is closed. You boldly walk on and go through the open door with Simon right behind you.

"Wow," you breath, as you take in the expansive space before you.

"Yeah," Simon agrees. "Obviously this was one of the main factory spaces," he says. It is mostly empty except for a few old and unidentifiable pieces of machinery and a few chairs scattered around. Thick wooden beams break the shadowed landscape here and there. The glass in another set of double doors at the far end of the room catches the beam from your flashlight and you start walking towards them. Then, you notice Simon is not with you.

You turn and see him standing near one of the pieces of equipment, the camera held loosely in his hand.

"Simon, what's going on?" you ask as you approach. When your flashlight crosses his face, he looks dazed. "Simon?" you say again, but he doesn't move.

"Simon!" you repeat, this time more urgently, and you grab his arm, but he remains motionless. You start to panic, unsure of what to do. Then, the door you had come through only minutes before suddenly slams shut. Your flashlight flickers and goes dark. The only light in the room now is the greenish glow from the viewfinder of the camera Simon still holds, casting a sickly, eerie look on his frozen face.

In the near-pitch-blackness, you hear a rustling noise somewhere behind you and what sounds like a footstep.

"H-hello? I-is someone h-h-here with us?" you say, unable to stop your voice from shaking. "Simon, what is wrong with you?" you whisper and nudge him with your elbow as you peer into the darkness for the source of the sounds. Again, you hear the rustling sound coming from behind you and you spin around, but you see nothing.

As you shove your dead flashlight in your pocket, you remember the walkie talkie clipped to your waist and reach for it. You press the button. "Jenna? Simon is… I don't know… I need your help," you say. You wait. The walkie responds with only static. "Hello, Jenna? I can't understand you. I need you to come help us," you repeat, only to get static in response.

"What am I going to do?" you say to yourself. "Okay, deep breath. I can go get help or I can try to break Simon out of this trance." You frown as you struggle to decide.

To go get help, go to page 78
To try to wake Simon from his trance, go to page 118

"Please! Help me!" Jenna yells again.

You shake yourself from your frozen state of fear and tug at the rope, but it doesn't budge. You pull and pull. Then you have an idea. "I'll go find Dave!"

"No! Don't leave me here!" she says but you are already heading down the stairs so fast you nearly fall several times. The whispering voices are all around you, but all you can do is ignore them. You must get Jenna help!

When you're back on the fourth level, you run down the hall and start shouting, "Dave! Josie! We need your help!"

You don't hear a response, so you head down the stairs as quickly as you can, shouting for Dave and Josie the whole way. At the top of the stairs from the third floor to the second floor, you think you hear Dave shouting back from below. You start down the stairs, your heart pounding out of your chest, your throat hurting from breathing hard and shouting in a panic. And then suddenly you are tumbling down the stairs. You hear something snap in your torso and then in one of your legs as you fall head over heels again and again. Your head bounces off the stairs several times until you finally come to a stop on the landing. Consciousness is fading fast as you blink. You see someone looming over you. Dave, maybe? But you have one last thought before you completely black out: someone grabbed your foot and made you fall.

Days later you wake from a coma with no memory of that night or of your friends who have all gone missing.

THE END

You look at Jenna and sigh, "I'm really sorry. I am so grateful that you guys wanted to be my friends and all, but I just don't think I can do this."

Jenna shrugs. "I wish you would stay, but I get it. This isn't for everyone. I guess we'll see you at school Monday."

"Okay. Thanks. Bye," you say. On your way to the front door, you see Josie in the kitchen with Rachel, Jenna's mom.

"Where are you going?" Josie asks.

You stop in the doorway. "I decided that this isn't really for me," you tell her.

"Oh, well, that's okay. It can be a bit overwhelming, especially with Jenna running the show," Josie says.

"Yeah. I guess. Okay, see you at school," you say.

"Bye!" You hear her say as the door closes behind you.

When you get home, you start to feel silly for bailing on your new friends, especially when they were really nice and understanding when you decided not to investigate. You distract yourself with homework – after all, you are new in school and have a lot of catching up to do.

Hours pass. Night falls. You stop your studying and wonder what your friends are up to, if they're having fun, if they're mad at you, if they need you.

Just then, your mom comes to your room. "Your father and I are going out for a late dinner. Want to come?"

If you want to go to dinner, go to page 27
If you want to stay home, go to page 26

Something tells you that whoever turned that light on, it wasn't Jenna or the others, so you turn away from it to go in search of them. Your eyes have adjusted to the dark now, and you look around you. Whoever was whispering before isn't there now.

You go in search of Jenna, Simon, Josie, and Dave. You decide to check the places you were supposed to investigate and remember that Jenna had said something about the second-floor break room, so you head up the stairs. As you move through a large room towards the hall that will lead to the room at the far end, you realize that you are being followed.

Then you hear a man's voice say, "I wouldn't go there if I were you."

You stop and turn around. You see a short broad man wearing a dark brown suit and a hat. His face is round and covered in acne scars. He scratches his big, bumpy nose with a chubby hand that holds a cigar, and his dark eyes squint at you. He looks unhappy but not scary.

"Why?" you ask.

"She doesn't like women. You're her competition. She won't like you," he says.

You turn back and look at the doorway and see a small woman with beady eyes and a pointed nose glaring at you.

"I see what you mean," you say. "Thank you."

"Her name is Ellie, and she's as nasty as they come. I'm Sam."

"Nice to meet you," you say, and tell him your name.

"You're a bit young to be here, though not the youngest. Sorry it happened to you the way it did," he says.

You frown. "Sorry *what* happened?" you ask.

"Huh," he grunts and shakes his head. "Death."

In that moment, you suddenly realize what he said is true, and it makes you feel dizzy. You black out, and when you come to, Sam is sitting next to you on the floor where your immortal form fell.

"Yeah, it can come as a shock," he says.

"But it all makes sense," you say. "I died when I fell down the stairs, didn't I?"

He nods. "Yes."

You frown again. "So… what do I do now?"

Sam extends a chubby hand, his cigar between his lips, and helps you up off the floor. "Allow me to show you around," he says.

You aren't sure how much time passes as Sam walks you around, introducing you to some of the other ghosts, warning you about others. You meet a small boy named Bobby, about nine years old but small for his age, who worked at the factory and died there when his arm got caught in a piece of machinery. It was torn from his body, and he bled to death. He walks around as a one-armed little boy ghost now.

"I learned how to move things," he tells you, beaming with pride. "I can open and close doors and hide things from the people who come here."

"Ah, a mischief maker, huh?" you say to him.

There are others, but as your afterlife falls into a strange routine, Sam and Bobby become your close friends. You spend the time – which passes nearly unnoticed – telling each other stories from your lives until you run out of stories, and then you start over.

Every once in a while, a few living people come by: people from town offices, police, homeless people looking for a place to sleep, and a realtor with a prospective buyer. But each time someone comes, you and the rest of the ghosts do everything you can to scare them away.

Then, one day, you are playing hide and seek with Bobby on the third floor when you hear voices coming from below. They are not the voices of the other ghosts that you've become accustomed to, but they are familiar. You and Bobby hover near the stairs and listen, then slowly descend. The voices are getting closer to the stairwell, and Bobby, always the prankster, finds a piece of debris on the floor and drops it down the stairs. It clatters and clanks and echoes as it tumbles. The people downstairs exclaim, and you hear them drawing quickly closer.

And then you hear your name being called.

If you run and hide, go to page 167
If you go towards the voices, go to page 39

"Actually, Sam is saying that we should go to the basement first, that there's something down there we should take care of before we do anything else," Josie says and starts walking.

"Like, a bad ghost?" you ask.

"I don't think so," she replies.

You frown and continue to follow her back through the large, open space. She stops again abruptly and smiles.

"What's happening?" you ask.

"Sam just introduced me to Bobby, a young boy who died while working here," she tells you.

"Oh, that's so sad," you say.

"Yes," she nods. "Sam and Bobby are friends, it seems, and they often play hide-and-seek all over the building. But Bobby's mischievous, and has been known to trip people, apparently."

"Noted," you say.

Josie continues on. She quickens her pace but turns back and says quietly, over her shoulder, "This is the room Bobby died in. His arm got stuck in a piece of equipment, tore it off, and he bled to death."

"Oh my god," you say in horror.

Josie shudders and hurries out of the room and down the stairs. You follow and as you come around on the landing, you see Jenna, Dave, and Simon on their way up.

"Hey! Look who decided to join us," Jenna says, with a nod to Simon.

"Hi," Josie says. "I thought you had a date?"

"She broke up with me," Simon mumbles and looks away.

"Oh, Simon, I'm really sorry. I know you liked her a lot," Josie says, but you sense just a hint of happiness in her tone.

"Thanks," he replies. You watch their eyes meet briefly and feel that a lot was said in their looks.

"So where are you guys heading?" Jenna asks.

"To the basement, and you guys should come with us," Josie says.

"But I have equipment I need to setup upstairs," Jenna says, almost whines.

"Well, Sam thinks it would be best if we did this all together, but you do what you want to do," Josie says.

"Do what together? Who is Sam?" Jenna asks, frowning.

"Come with us, and I'll tell you," Josie replies. Jenna rolls her eyes at Josie, but Josie says, "Well? What will you do?"

If Jenna continues setup, go to page 97
If everyone goes to the basement, go to page 120

"Whoa!" you shout, and another plate goes flying across the room. You follow it in the viewfinder of the camera. "Jenna is going to freak!"

"Yes, she is!" Josie agrees, shouting over the sound of breaking glass as another dish smashes.

"Josie, what are you seeing? Or sensing?" you ask.

"It's definitely Ellie doing this," she says. "She bullied and intimidated in life, and she's still trying to bully and intimidate in death."

"It's working," you say, glad your feet feel glued to the floor, or you might run from the building.

"Don't let her get to you," Josie says. "She *wants* you to be afraid and if you give in to that, you give her exactly what she wants and that gives her power."

"How can I *not* be afraid?" you ask with complete seriousness.

"The best way is to remove the fear. Logic can help with that. Or laughter."

"Laughter?" you reply.

"Yeah!" Josie says. "Okay. What's a ghost's favorite makeup to wear?"

You shrug.

"Mas-scare-ah!" She laughs at herself. You giggle, mostly at her. Then she says, "What room does a ghost not need in a house? A living room!" She laughs again and you join in. "Why do ghosts love elevators?" she asks.

"I don't know," you say with a shrug.

"It lifts their spirits!" she replies and breaks into a bigger fit of laughter and soon you are both laughing so hard you are holding your stomachs. When the laughter subsides, Josie says to you, "How do you feel now?"

You nod. "Yeah, definitely less afraid. And it feels different in here. Not as heavy."

"I agree. I think Ellie has finished her performance for now, so let's keep going," Josie replies and heads out of the room and back down the hall.

You follow her to the stairwell and climb to the third floor. Like the first floor, there is one long hallway, pock-marked by the gaping black holes that are the doorways into the various rooms, highlighted by Josie's flashlight.

You and Josie move slowly down the hall. "Are we still being followed by that guy?" you ask.

"Yes, but he's keeping his distance for now," she replies.

Moments later, you see movement in the shadows just outside the beam of the flashlight and look at the small screen of the camera's viewfinder just in time to see what looks like a small figure dashing across the hallway. You and Josie both stop in your tracks.

"Did you see that?" you say.

"Yes, you saw it too?" she asks.

"Yes! I saw just movement with my eyes, but in the camera, it looked like a little boy!" you tell her.

"I saw a little boy, too," she says, though she doesn't sound happy about it. She turns around and stares back into the darkness from which you came.

"Josie?" you say. "What's happening?"

"We need to get out of here," she says. "Come on." And she heads back towards the stairs. You hurry after her and hear footsteps behind you. Glancing over your shoulder, you see nothing, so you point the camera back, and in the viewfinder, you see a small form running after you.

At the stairwell, Josie pauses, looks up into the darkness of the fourth floor above, and then looks down into the equally dark darkness of the lower levels below.

If you and Josie go up, go to page 140
If you and Josie go down, go to page 92

Josie starts up the stairs and you follow behind her with Simon right on your heels. The stairs are narrow and steep, and they creak under everyone's feet. Your heart starts to pound in anticipation of what may lie at the top.

You reach the top and enter the tower room. It is a large, square space with high windows and a high vaulted ceiling, with thick beams crisscrossing. Hanging from the center of the X formed by the beams is a rope that ends in a noose about five feet above your head. There is also an old, rusty metal twin bed with a bare and stained mattress in one corner, garbage strewn everywhere – fast food wrappers, beer cans and alcohol bottles, and dirty, discarded clothing – and graffiti covering every wall.

"I don't like this," Simon says as all three of you shine your flashlights around the room, taking in the subject-matter of the graffiti. You see pentagrams, a cartoonish devil face, bubble numbers '666' in multiple places, and layers of other graphic and grotesque images of death and destruction. In one spot, someone has written "I summon the demon" but the word that came next is mostly covered by an alien face, a gray oval with large black eyes and a small slit for a mouth grinning mischievously at you.

Then you notice the red light blinking from one of Jenna's cameras, watching you, and it makes you feel a little better knowing she has already been there.

"Okay, Josie, can you tell me what you are picking up on here?" you ask.

Josie turns to face the camera. "First, I'd like to know if Simon is feeling anything," she says.

You turn the camera to focus on Simon. He has a deep scowl on his face, and he is staring at the ground. "Simon?" you prompt him.

"I don't know," he says, swallowing hard. "I just feel kinda sick to my stomach all of a sudden and I feel really, I don't know, jumpy, like I'm gonna jump out of my skin any second now. And now my head is starting to feel… it feels fuzzy, like when you take medicine that makes you drowsy, but you have to stay awake."

"Would you like to know why you feel that way?" Josie asks him.

"Ugh, not really, but tell me anyway," he says.

Josie smiles and tilts her head at Simon. "There is a guy standing right behind you, Simon, who overdosed up here, and he's not quite sure what is going on. He is rather frantic and twitchy."

"And you can feel that, Simon?" you ask.

"Unfortunately," he replies.

"Can you tell us anything else?" you ask Josie.

She is quiet for a few minutes, and then she finally says, "I think he may have been affected by the ghosts when he was alive, probably saw and heard them, but with the highs and lows of his drug and drinking habit, I don't think he realized he was being haunted. I don't think he knows that he's still being haunted."

"Weird," you say.

"A little," Josie nods.

"And is he responsible for this, um, artwork?" you ask.

She shakes her head. "I think ignorant living people did that, with no clue as to the possible implications."

"So, is this area… dangerous?" you ask.

Just then, there is a flurry of shadow movement and Simon cries out. When you finally get the camera on him, you see the rope from the noose has wound itself around his torso and is in the process of curling around his neck like a snake.

"Simon!" Josie yells.

"Help! Me!" he chokes out.

Josie goes to him and tugs on the rope. "Put the camera down and help me!" she yells to you.

You jump and set the camera down on a small table in the corner, and rush to help. You and Josie tug and tug until finally the rope relaxes and falls to the floor. Simon clutches at his throat as he gasps for breath.

"Are you okay?" Josie asks.

"Yeah," he says through breaths, rubbing at the rope burns on his neck.

"Should we get you out of here?" you ask.

If you leave the tower, go to page 54
If you stay, go to page 60

"I'm as ready as I'll ever be," you say to Jenna with a sigh and a forced smile.

"Awesome! Then I think we are ready to head over there. I'll just pack this stuff up and we'll get going," she says.

You help them load everything into the trunk of Dave's car and everyone piles in. Jenna is in the front seat, navigating for Dave.

"Who needs GPS when you have me?" Jenna says with a bright smile at her boyfriend.

The roads he takes are dark and unfamiliar to you. Josie is sitting beside you, and you want to talk to her, but she has her fists clenched in her lap and is staring out the window, angled away from you. You want to ask questions about the building, but you remember that Jenna doesn't want Josie to know anything about the location before you get there. You start to wonder if you made a mistake in continuing on with the investigation, though it's clearly too late to change your mind.

Then Dave turns and pulls to a stop in a parking lot. Jenna jumps out of the car, and you follow a little more reluctantly. Looking around, you see a sea of potholes and broken pavement with weeds growing up through the cracks. Looming just ahead is a four-story towering brick monster with dozens of black eyes that stare into your soul.

"What do you guys think?" Jenna says to you, Dave, and Josie with an eager grin.

"What did you get us into?" Josie asks.

You chuckle, thinking she's teasing, but then you look at her face. She's pale, and her eyes are wide as she looks up at the building. You wonder if she's already sensing ghosts inside.

"Well, that's what we're here to find out," Jenna replies, undeterred. She starts pulling her equipment bags from the trunk. "Let's get inside. Dave, do you have the key?"

"Sure do, Babe," he says, pulling keys from his pocket.

You grab a bag and follow Jenna and Dave as they walk towards the building, and Josie trails behind you. They enter through a door at the side and go into a small room. Dave flips a switch next to the door and a fluorescent light flickers to life overhead. There's a long table against one wall where Jenna puts stuff.

"Okay, first things first." From one of the bags, she pulls out several black armbands and hands one to everyone. She then pulls out a small case. She unzips it, and starts handing out silver, rectangular audio recorders. "These go on your left arm," she says of the armband, "and the recorders go inside. Just hit the power button on the side, and then record. It all should be ready to go."

You do as the others are doing and strap the band around your arm. Jenna then pulls out a video camera from a bag and turns to you.

"Do you want to go with Josie and record her as she does her walk-through? Or would you rather stay with me and help set up the rest of the equipment?"

If you go with Josie, go to page 65
If you help Jenna with setup, go to page 47

"No thanks, Mom. I need to finish homework," you say.

"Okay. Well, there's leftover lasagna from last night if you get hungry," she says.

"Thanks," you say.

Another hour passes and you get drowsy. You fall asleep working on a paper for history class, and you don't wake up when Jenna calls your cell phone to plead for help.

THE END

You sit at dinner, picking at your food, feeling guilty for abandoning your new friends. Being in a new school was tougher than you had imagined, but then Jenna befriended you, introducing you to Josie, Dave, Simon, and lots of other people. You stopped being "the new kid" thanks to them.

You fiddle with your cell phone, debating whether or not you should text Jenna and tell her you have changed your mind, but you're still not entirely sure. Would they even want you back? Would they ignore your call?

Maybe I'm just not cut out for this stuff, you think to yourself. You've already bailed on them once. Can you really handle it? Can you handle sitting in the dark, talking to the air, waiting for some unseen force to do something? When you think of it like that, it all sounds rather silly and not something to be afraid of. You start to feel confident that you could do this, and you feel bad for not sticking with it, despite that little part of you that is still terrified.

If you text Jenna, go to page 36
If you decide not to text Jenna, go to page 63

"Yeah, let's call them," Josie says. "I don't want to have to repeat myself on this one."

Simon tosses Josie the walkie. She presses the button and says, "Jenna, Dave. We're down in the basement and I've found something unusual. Can you come down here so I can try to explain it to everyone?"

"On our way!" Jenna replies.

Simon walks towards you and asks, "How's your ankle?"

You flex it and roll it. "Better," you reply.

"Let's have you try to stand on it," he says and helps steady you as you rise from the stairs. There is a little twinge of pain when you put your weight on your foot, but it no longer feels unable to hold you. "That's good. But you should rest it a bit longer, just to be safe," he says.

"Okay," you say and return to your perch on the stairs.

"You okay, Josie?" Simon calls over his shoulder.

"Mmm hmm," she replies from her place in the dark, in her own personal spotlight from her flashlight. You can tell she's focusing on something.

"Are your investigations always like this?" you ask him.

"Not really," he replies.

Just then, you hear feet thundering down the stairs, echoing from above your head. Even though you're sure it is Jenna and Dave, you feel the desire to stand and move away from the stairwell… just in case.

"Is it me or does it sound like a thousand people are coming down the stairs?" Josie asks.

"It's not you," Simon says.

You're relieved that they are thinking what you are thinking. "Maybe the other ghosts are coming with them," you say, and chuckle, but the look on Simon's face tells you that he is taking the possibility seriously. Suddenly your heart jumps into double-time with nerves, and you imagine a few dozen gauzy specters hurrying down the stairs behind an oblivious Jenna and Dave.

But when Jenna and Dave arrive in the basement, if there are any ghosts with them, you are unfortunately unable to see them. "What's going on?" Jenna asks, breathless but her voice filled with curious excitement   .

You move slowly, your ankle feeling better by the minute, and make your way over to where everyone else is gathering around Josie. Josie brings Jenna and Dave up to speed about following the apparition into a room on the fourth floor, sensing the odd energy, and trailing it down to the basement. She repeats what she had said earlier, "This is unlike anything I've encountered before, and you are all going to think I'm insane, but hear me out."

"I'm beyond intrigued," Jenna says. "Please, go on!"

Josie takes a deep breath in and does a gesture with her arms in a gesture distinctive of ballet dancers. "Okay, so, this column of energy… is alive. Like, it has a consciousness, an awareness of its own."

Your jaw drops, and you can see in the lights of everyone's flashlights that they too are staring at Josie's words in amazement.

"So, what you are saying is that there is a column of energy here that can think for itself?" Simon asks.

"Essentially, yes," Josie replies. "And by the way, it doesn't like us."

Just then, the ground below your feet rumbles. You've never been in an earthquake before, but you think it must feel just like this.

"Um, guys… what do we do?" you ask.

If you run, go to page 35
If you stay, go to page 179

"Can you tell us why? And do we have to go so fast?" you ask as you hurry up the stairs. Josie and Simon both move quickly but you are huffing and puffing after only a few steps.

"Because I now have Sam, Bobby, and Edward dogging me and I want to finish this walk-through so I can focus on crossing everyone over," she says, clearly growing more irritated by the minute.

Simon also sees this in Josie, and as you finally reach the landing of the third floor, Simon is standing with Josie, one hand on each of her shoulders and he is looking into her eyes. "Josie, take a breath," he says. "You can do this. Tell them – Sam, Bobby, Edward – what you need from them in order to hang out with us. Your rules. Your boundaries."

Josie takes a deep inhale and lets it out, then another. She visibly relaxes and as you look at the two of them through the viewfinder of the camera, you see what looks like tiny electric sparks passing between them. *Probably just dust*, you think.

Then, Josie says to the air, "Sam, Bobby, and Edward, I need all of you to back off. Sam, I have given you permission to help us with the work we are doing here, but I need you to be respectful of my energy and my space. Bobby and Edward, you can hang out with us, but only if you promise to be quiet for now."

You give her a few beats and then ask, "Did they agree?"

"Yes," she says with a sigh of relief. "And they apologized. Thank you, Simon," she says with a smile. He nods and takes a big step back from her. You check the viewfinder again but no longer see the little sparkling lights between them. The spell has been broken for now.

"Alright, so what is going on here?" you ask.

Josie takes a few steps down the hall, stops, and turns back to you and Simon. "It's really quiet up here, actually," she says.

"Is that because there are no spirits here?" you ask.

Josie nods. "At least, not right now. That's one of the common misconceptions about ghosts, that they stay stuck and haunting just one room in a house or building, but that is almost never the case. They can move around as they please if they believe they can. And I suspect, with everything we're doing here, that all the spirits have been attracted to the other levels, wherever there is human activity happening right now."

"Okay, so… what do you want to do?" you ask.

"Let's go up to the fourth level," she says, and heads for the stairs.

Just as you turn to follow her, you see what looks like a dark form of a head, shoulders, and torso peek out of the doorway nearby, and then disappear back inside the room. You open your mouth to say something but decide it must have been your eyes playing tricks on you because Josie seems to really know what she's doing. You hurry to catch up to Josie and Simon.

When you join them on the fourth floor, Josie is standing in the hallway in front of a closed door. She shines her light down the hallway, and you can see that the other doors are open.

She shakes her head. "There is someone very bad in that room. Sam says it's his old boss. Yes… a *very* bad person."

"Are we going in there?" you ask as she starts walking down the hall, away from the closed door.

"Not yet," she replies. She stops in the doorway to the room opposite the closed door. "That portal that's downstairs… it has been active up here too. It's calm right now but I think people may have experienced things happening in this room."

You and Simon follow Josie as she zigzags down the hall to peek into the different rooms. You are about halfway down the hall when you see a flashing streak of something move past the camera and then you hear a small, metallic plink.

"What was that?" you say.

"It sounded metallic," Simon says.

"I agree," you and Josie say at the same time.

"I think whatever it was landed over here," Simon says, walking back in the direction you had just come, shining his flashlight along the floor. "Hey, this could be it! A penny!" he says. He picks it up and tosses it in the air. When it hits the floor again, he says, "That sounds like what I heard."

"Me, too," you say. "Josie, are you getting any… readings from this? Or information from Sam?"

Josie nods. "Pennies from heaven," she says.

"What?" you say.

"It's a song," Simon says.

"Yes, and it is also something that is commonly reported with hauntings, but usually when a loved one is involved," Josie says. "Like a beloved grandmother. Whenever you're thinking of her, suddenly you'll find a penny on the ground. Some people have even reported that the pennies always have the same year on them, whether it's their birth year or the year of their loved one's death, it can be significant."

"But why here? None of us have a dead loved one haunting this building," you say. Then, "Or, do we?"

Josie shakes her head. "No, we don't but the person who threw the penny believed in that, and she's trying to do it to let us know she's here."

"Why do I find that really sad?" you say.

"It is sad," Simon says. "I'd guess she is sad and lonely."

"Are you guessing? Or…." Josie says.

"What does that mean?" you ask.

"Oh, Simon's an Empath," Josie says.

"What's an Empath?" you ask.

"Can we add that to your list of questions to be answered later?" Simon says. "We should get on with the walk-through."

Josie chuckles and you think you can see Simon's cheeks flushing even in the darkness and night vision. "Bobby likes to play up here, but he doesn't like the guy in the tower," Josie says, continuing on as though she hadn't pushed one of Simon's buttons. She points to a dark doorway that is different from the rest. In your viewfinder, you can see the beginning of a narrow staircase just beyond the threshold.

"Who is the guy in the tower?" you ask, half-expecting to see a gruesome face peek out from the darkness.

"Shall we go up and find out?" Josie asks, looking from you to Simon and back.

If you go up to the tower, go to page 71
If you finish the 4th floor, go to page 88

"Let's get out of here!" Dave yells and everyone hurries towards the stairs. You follow after them, your ankle still smarting just a bit, so you struggle and fall behind.

Jenna stops partway up the stairs and turns, saying, "Wait! My equipment!"

Dave opens his mouth to protest and reaches to grab her just as another rumble starts. The stairs tremor violently underneath your feet, and a strange groaning, crunching sound comes from above.

The side wall of the building and the floors above your head collapse onto the five of you. It happens so fast that all of you are dead before you can think about it.

You see darkness, and then a very bright light in a color you struggle to name, and then… nothing.

THE END

With a sigh, you open your text app and write: "Hi Jenna. Sorry I bailed. I'd like to come help if you still need me."

Butterflies flutter in your stomach as you hit send. What if she says no? What if she doesn't answer at all?

"Are you okay? You don't look good," your mom says.

"I'm fine. But I think I really messed things up with my new friends," you say.

Then your phone buzzes to signal a new message. It is a text from Jenna that says, "Yes! Come right away! 25 Maple Street. Hurry!"

You then beg your parents to leave the restaurant and drop you off on their way home. After lots of pleading that your entire social future at your new school depends on it, they reluctantly agree. On the drive over, you are nervous and excited, and determined not to chicken out again. Your eyes are glued to the GPS as it navigates your dad through unfamiliar streets, and you can see your destination growing closer and closer. Your nerves are overloading, and you feel like you might lose your dinner.

And then you're there.

"Wow, this place looks... spooky!" Dad says, looking out the windshield at the immense building in front of him.

"Dad, that's not helpful," you say, rolling your eyes, but silently you admit he is right. The building is a four-story towering brick monster with dozens of black eyes that seem to be staring into your soul.

"Have fun and be safe!" Mom calls after you as you climb from the car. Then headlights flash across the whole scene – your car, the looming brick structure, the sad, wilting bushes along the front – as another car comes to a stop in the parking lot next to you. Simon gets out of the car.

"Hey, I thought you were already here," he says to you.

You flush with embarrassment as you admit, "I bailed earlier but decided I should come help them."

"Awesome. She called me in for back-up, too. I guess things are getting interesting already. Are you ready to go inside?"

You look at your mom and dad and wave as they drive off. "I'm as ready as I'll ever be."

You follow Simon to a side door and enter a small room where you are immediately accosted by Jenna.

"I'm so glad you guys are here. This place is crazy! But I'm not going to tell you anything now. I want you guys to see if you experience any of it for yourselves," she says with a knowing grin. "First, though, you need to put these on."

She hands you both a small, silver, rectangular audio recorder and a black Velcro armband. You watch Simon insert the recorder into the armband and strap it to his left arm and you do the same, noticing that Jenna also has one strapped to her arm.

Jenna answers your question before you ask. "We all wear audio recorders that we have running at all times. That way when the investigation is over, we can sync the recorders and video to help us know where everyone was during the night and who made what sounds. It helps eliminate false evidence of EVPs and shadows and things. It also increases our chances of capturing an EVP since, theoretically, they can happen at any time."

"So, you don't just sit and do EVP sessions like they do on the TV shows?" you ask.

"Well, yeah, we do, but those don't always result in evidence. We've had EVP's show up on our recorders when we're just walking through a place chatting like we normally do. And I don't want to risk missing any evidence."

"That makes sense," you reply, nodding.

"Alright, Boss," Simon says to Jenna. "What's our assignments?"

"Okay, you have two choices. Dave and Josie are downstairs in the basement. You two can either go up to the tower and investigate together, or I can get the other two back up here and we can regroup and split up from there. What do you guys want to do?"

Simon speaks up first. "I think we should get the other two up here and let's regroup."

"Okay, what do you think?" Jenna asks you.

If you want to investigate with Simon, go to page 136
If you want to regroup, go to page 56

"Jenna? Josie?" you say.

"I think I heard my name," Josie says. You see her step into view at the bottom of the stairs, and then she calls out, "Hello! Are you there? I think I heard you say my name. We're here to apologize to you, and to help… if you'll allow us."

You frown at these people who were once your friends and walk down the stairs towards them. It's the four of them: Josie, Jenna, Simon, and Dave. They look older, but you're not sure how old. You have no idea how much time has actually passed since you went on an investigation with them and died, to be left behind in this place by them.

"Want me to throw something else at them?" Bobby asks.

"Not yet," you say to him. "But maybe."

"Who are you talking to? Who wants to throw things at us?" Josie says to you.

"She can hear us," Bobby says, with a childish snarl.

"Yeah, it's weird, right?" you say to him.

"Yes, I can hear you," Josie says and starts to climb the stairs towards you. "And I can see you," she says.

You look at her. It's a weird sensation, being looked at, heard, acknowledged by a living person. It's been so long.

"What do you all want?" you snap. "Do you want me and my friends to play for you? Perform for you like trained monkeys? 'Hey, you, Ghost! Knock on a wall for us!' Pshaw!"

"That's not why we're here," Josie says. You can see her cheeks burning.

"You feel guilty, don't you," you say, feeling a little satisfied.

She nods. "Yes, actually. We all do. We are so sorry for what happened to you."

"We are so sorry!" Jenna says from behind Josie, stifling a sob as Dave pulls her into him. "I never thought something like that would happen in a million years!"

"But it did happen," you say.

"She was torn apart by what happened to you," Josie says. "We all were. We all witnessed you die. We were helpless. It was awful."

"I feel so sorry for them. Whaa! Whaa! Whaa!" says Bobby, who starts laughing. His childish laugh echoes off the walls, and you see the faces of the living people react in fear when they hear it.

You laugh at them, too, but you notice Josie squinting at Bobby, and then her eyes go wide. She looks at you again.

"Thick as thieves, the two of you?" she says.

"Something like that," you tell her.

She shakes her head and frowns, and you wonder why. "Can you please come down here so we can talk to you?"

"Don't go with *them*," Bobby sneers. "They're gross, stupid living people."

You look at him, sitting on one of the stairs, looking small. "They were my friends once. I owe it to them to hear them out," you say.

He stands. "Ha! You died because of *them*! But have it your way!" He runs off, his laughter echoing again. You see Simon and Jenna shiver.

You slowly make your way down the stairs to the people who became your friends when you were new in school and stand at the spot where you died.

"Is this supposed to be ironic?" you ask Josie, indicating where you are all standing.

"No, it's necessary," she replies.

"For what?" you ask.

"For crossing you over," she says.

Fear grips your heart, and your eyes widen. "Why would you want to do that? To appease your guilty consciences?"

"You have every right to be angry with us. We brought you here that night, and you died because you were here with us. We are guilty of your death, at least in part, but that's not why you should cross over," she says.

You frown and step closer to her. You haven't encountered many living people since your death, and usually you were just trying to frighten them. But now, you are curious. You feel these living people in a way you didn't when you were alive. You feel Josie's sincerity and there is a groundedness to her that you haven't felt before from anyone.

"What do you mean, 'at least in part'?" you ask, as you weave through Jenna, Simon, and Dave, feeling their energy as well. Dave radiates compassion and sadness but Jenna reeks of despair and guilt. Simon's energy feels like humility and regret. You circle back to face Josie.

"I mean that we aren't the only ones involved in your death," she says.

"Are you blaming me?" you ask, horrified.

"No!" she responds quickly. "I was referring to the ghost that tripped you."

This information hits you like a bucket of ice water being dumped over your head. "Who tripped me?" you ask.

"You really don't know?" Josie asks you.

You feel suddenly deflated. "I never thought about it. I just thought I fell down the stairs."

Josie shakes her head. "It wasn't an accident. I don't believe that he meant for you to die, just to cause trouble...."

"You don't mean…?" but the instant she said it, you knew who it was.

Josie just looks at you, pity in her eyes.

Suddenly, you call out, "Bobby! Bobby, get back here!"

Tension zips through the air so quickly that you hear Jenna say, "Oh… what *is* that?"

Josie replies, "That's the arrival of the trouble-maker ghost that caused our friend to fall down the stairs."

"Wow," Simon says with a shiver.

Bobby comes slowly down the stairs towards you, a sheepish grin on his face. "It was you?" you say to him. "All this time we've hung out, played, been friends, and it was you?"

He shrugs at you, and you realize that he is a conundrum; having died as a child but then existing in spirit form for decades gives him an odd imbalance of immaturity and wisdom. You want to be mad, but all you feel for him is sadness.

"I'm not mad at you, Bobby," you say.

"You should be," he says.

"Bobby." Josie says his name in a calm and warm tone that catches his attention. He moves closer to her. "You're unhappy here, aren't you? Happy people don't hurt others."

He shrugs again.

"It's okay, Bobby. We're all unhappy. That's why we're here. Being unhappy together has made it a little better, though, right?" you say.

He nods.

"Bobby, there's someone who has been looking for you for a long time, someone who has been waiting to talk to you for a really long time," Josie says.

"Really? Who?" he asks.

Josie gestures to the nearby wall where suddenly a bright square of swirling foggy light appears like a doorway. You can see a figure moving closer, getting bigger, as it approaches through this portal until you are looking at a young man who looks like an older version of Bobby.

"Michael?" Bobby says, his voice small.

"It's me, little brother," the young man says. "Remember the time we stole the bowl of icing from the counter when Mother wasn't looking, and we ran to the pond and ate the whole thing before she found us?"

Bobby laughs. Again, it echoes, and the others hear it. "That was one of the best days," Bobby says.

"We can have more days like that, if you come with me," Michael says to Bobby.

Josie then says, "It's time for you to go, Bobby. You don't belong here. You never did."

Bobby looks at you. "I really am sorry," he says. "I don't know if it's right if I leave you."

You smile at him. "It's your time, Bobby. And someday, it will be my time," you tell him. "It's okay. Go."

He hesitates, then smiles, and walks to his brother, taking his outstretched hand. The foggy light swirls and grows bright before disappearing in a blink and Michael and Bobby are gone.

"You were very kind to him," Josie says to you.

You shrug. "What good does it do to hold a grudge."

"Exactly," Josie smiles. "I knew you were ready," she says.

You aren't surprised. You felt it the moment the words left your lips – the change in the air around you, the change in the energy that makes up your form. You feel the warmth of a love so deep and pure that you want to weep with joy. You feel it pulling you, drawing you closer to it and away from them. But before you go, you have a message for Josie and your friends. As if you are looking through a brightly lit tunnel of fog, Josie turns to the others and relays your message: "Thank you for being my friend. You made moving to a new town painless. I do not regret a thing, and I don't want any of you to regret anything either. Goodbye!"

"Goodbye! Thank you!" Jenna calls and waves at the air. The others do the same, but you are far away, finally in the lovely oblivion of perfect peace.

THE END

"I'm really sorry to do this, guys," you say, "but I don't think I can do this. I want to go home."

"Oh," Josie says. "Okay. Yeah, that's totally okay."

"Yeah. I wouldn't do this if it wasn't for my friends. I get it," Simon says.

"Thanks," you say, your cheeks burning with embarrassment again.

"I'll walk you downstairs," Simon says.

"No, that's okay. Stay with Josie. I'm sure I can get to the equipment room fine," you say. "It will be my final act for the investigation. But will you guys break it to Jenna for me?"

"Sure. No problem," Josie says.

"Thanks. Bye," you say. With a deep breath, you turn and head back to the stairs. You are still terrified, the dark beyond the beam of your flashlight seems even darker and more menacing than before. You hurry, but not too fast. You don't want to fall.

You reach the first floor with no issues, and immediately find your cell phone to call your mom. You give her the address and you can hear the car keys in her hand before she hangs up the call. You are immediately relieved.

You remove the recorder from your arm and decide to wait outside. Though the equipment room isn't as scary as the rest of the place, you don't want to be inside that building any longer. You wait near Dave's car, but time passes slowly, and you start to get nervous again. You keep checking your phone in case your mom calls or texts, but the screen is blank. You turn in circles in your impatience. At one point you see a flashlight in a window on the 2nd floor and realize it must be Jenna and Dave. You feel bad for bailing, but the relief you still feel tells you that you made the right decision.

Again, you turn in a circle, and again your eye is caught by something – this time, it is a little blue light dancing out over the swamp.

"Uh-uh!" you shout. "You can't have me!"

Oddly, the light fades and disappears.

Moments later, your mother's car pulls in and you can hardly jump in the car fast enough. "I have never been so happy to see you!" you say. "Please get me out of here!"

THE END

"I'll stay and help you set up," you tell Jenna.

"Okay," she smiles and hands Dave the camera. "Well, Dave, it's up to you to do the walk-through with Josie. You know how it goes."

"You got it, Babe," he says, lays a kiss on her cheek, and he and Josie then disappear through the door at the far end of the room into the darkness beyond.

"Okay, so I have four other cameras," Jenna says. "I want two of them in the basement where the man was seen, one in the tower, and the other one we'll carry as we walk around and investigate."

"What do you need me to do?" you ask Jenna.

"Grab that bag, and follow me," she says, also picking up an equipment bag. She hands you a flashlight and heads for the door Josie and Dave disappeared through not long before. You follow nervously as Jenna strides confidently down the long, dark hallway. You're on your guard, expecting at any moment that something – or someone – will jump out of the shadows to get you. But it is quiet. All you hear are the soft pads of your and Jenna's sneakered feet as you walk down the hall. You don't even see or hear Josie and Dave. You find it eerily quiet, but Jenna seems unconcerned.

"Where do you think Josie and Dave went?" you ask, surprised at how your voice echoes around you.

"I'm not sure," Jenna replies in a whisper. "I don't hear them at all."

"Me either," you say, also whispering this time.

Jenna stops and you stop beside her. She is shining her light down into the large rectangular hole of the stairwell leading to the basement level. Partially blocking it is the rise of the stairs going to the second floor.

"Does this place have an elevator?" you ask.

"No, but even if it did, I don't think it would be safe to use." Jenna stands at the very edge of the stairs descending into the basement. Her light doesn't reach the bottom.

A shiver runs up your body.

"Okay, down we go!" says Jenna.

You reluctantly follow her down into the darkness. "What is it about basements always being so spooky?" you ask.

"I know, right?" agrees Jenna. "I can't even begin to tell you how many hauntings I've read about where there was activity in the basement."

The space is large and mostly open and empty except for large posts set at regular intervals, likely at least partially responsible for keeping the building standing. What little ambient light that made its way into the upper floor windows from nearby light posts outside was not able to find a single hole or window into the basement. It has that smell most basements have of mustiness combined with years and years of dust which makes you sneeze.

"Bless you," Jenna says. She starts to pull equipment from her bag.

"Thank you. What can I do to help?" you ask.

"I'll set this camera up here by the stairs. There's another one in the bag you have. Why don't you set it up on the other side of the room," she says, pointing away from her into the dark abyss of the basement.

"O-okay," you say, and you walk the long walk to the other side of the room, scanning the darkness with your flashlight the whole time.

You make quick work of setting up the tripod and attaching the camera to the top, glad that Jenna isn't there to see your hands shaking with nerves. You are looking for the power button when a shadow breaks the beam of your flashlight.

"Jenna?" you say, assuming – hoping – it was her.

"What?" she asks, her voice coming from the other side of the room. You then realize you can see her in the light of her own flashlight, still near the stairwell.

"Um…." You're trying to speak, but another shadow cuts the beam of your flashlight, and then another. You start to panic. You try to shout for Jenna, but your voice won't come out of your mouth.

"Jenna!" You finally say but your voice catches, it is too quiet, and Jenna is too far. You try again and squeak out, "Je—" and that is when a man's head appears before you. His face is ashen, his eyes sunken, and his mouth is a gaping hole. He gets in your face and screams, "Get out!"

If you scream and run from the room, go to page 59
If you stand your ground, go to page 102

In the equipment room, Jenna turns on the light, momentarily blinding everyone. "Sorry!" she says. Before your eyes can adjust, the door to the outside opens, startling you, but it is Simon, Jenna's older brother. "I'm so glad everyone's here to help! Okay, we have five of us now. I don't want anyone investigating on their own. This building is too big and there are potential hazards like things to trip on or wonky floors, so I want us to stick together. One team of two and one team of three. How does that sound?"

Everyone nods their agreement.

"Alright. Josie, have you finished your walk-through?" Jenna asks.

"Yes, and I have to say, I cannot believe this place exists," Josie says. "Where do you want me to start?"

"Oh, I almost forgot! I baked cookies!" Jenna says. She pulls a plastic tub from one of the bags and lifts the lid. The smell of butter and chocolate and brown sugar instantly hits you. She passes the tub after taking a cookie for herself and says, "Start at the beginning."

Josie takes a bite of cookie and starts: "There's a *ton* of energy here. The toil of the workers and the demands of the management are soaked into every inch of this place. And there are a lot of ghosts. Some don't know they are dead so they wouldn't talk to me, but others were chatty."

"Excellent!" Jenna says.

"Yes, it certainly makes my job easier," Josie chuckles. "So, I'll start from the top and work my way down. First, in the tower, is Corey, the homeless guy. It does seem like he accidentally OD'd, but I think he was being harassed by some of the ghosts and that kind of drove him to it. Like, normally, the drugs would drown out the voices in his head, but this time, the drugs didn't work because it wasn't voices in his head. But he didn't know that, so he took more and more until… you know…. He's not very nice and tried to grope me."

"What?" Simon exclaims, standing suddenly and sending half a cookie sliding across the floor, while you and Jenna exchange knowing glances.

"It's okay, Simon. One of Dave's Guides restrained him," she says, and he sits again.

"Can I ask a question?" you interrupt.

"Of course," says Josie.

"What do you mean by 'one of Dave's Guides'?" you ask.

"Oh, I was referring to his Spirit Guide, a spirit that is with him to guide him in life. We all have them," she says.

"We do?"

"Yeah," Josie nods and smiles.

"Can we talk about Guides later? I'd like to get back to who we're dealing with here," Jenna says.

Josie lets out a huff of air and says, "Okay, so fourth floor… there's a man who I believe was the owner of this place when it was first built and operating. I think his office was up there, so he mostly stays up there. He shows himself as a tall, slender shadow-figure. He doesn't like that we are here. I sense that he is hiding some secrets."

"Did you get a name?" Jenna asks.

"Jeffrey, I think. I didn't get a last name," Josie replies, then goes on. "On the third floor I encountered a spirit that had kind of been following us around most of the night but was finally able to draw him out. His name is Bobby, and he died at 9 years old when his arm got stuck in a piece of equipment back when, you know, they would allow young children to work in factories. He's a bit of a mischief-maker, I think, so be careful. He runs all over this place and likes to play hide-and-seek. He seems to have befriended Sam, a man who was a manager here, I think, not at the same time as when Bobby died. He seems to try to keep an eye on things around here – Sam does – and they do their best to avoid Jeffrey.

"On the second floor, in the breakroom, is Ellie Watson, a black-widow-type woman who preyed on lonely men. She stole their money and their lives, from what I can tell. She didn't like me at all and started throwing plates and things."

"She's the one that made the mess?" Jenna asks.

"Yup. And at least one of her victims is hanging around up there though I doubt many people experience him. His name is Martin.

"On this level I encountered a couple more workers, a father and son duo – Edward and Edward Junior who they called Eddie – who don't know they're dead. They still think they are here to do their jobs. I think they were the ones moving things around on the construction crew – although Bobby probably did some of it, too – but they weren't being mischievous, they just thought the stuff was in the way or put in the wrong place.

"Then, in the basement, is a nasty guy who I think angered the wrong person with his attitude and ended up dead and dumped out back in the swamp, but he hangs out in the basement area and tries to scare people as much as he can."

"Wow, that's amazing," Jenna says.

"Thanks," Josie replies. She grabs another cookie and takes a bite. "We're only partly through the night and I'm exhausted."

"Well, rest up for a few minutes, and then we can split up and get this investigation going," Jenna says.

Dave passes out bottles of water to everyone and then you realize you need to use the bathroom.

You whisper this to Jenna who says, "Oh, right, I think I forgot to tell you. The only option is a port-a-potty outside from the construction crew."

You make a face of mild disgust and consider if your need is *that* urgent, but nerves have gotten to you, and you know that if you wait, it will only get worse. "I gotta go," you say with a shrug and head out the door. You let your eyes adjust to the darkness outside and you see the port-a-potty in a shadowy corner of the parking lot.

"What the heck was I thinking…," you wonder aloud as you hurry across the broken pavement. You take a deep breath and hold it, pull open the plastic door, and hurry inside. It is difficult – holding a flashlight while holding your breath and trying to do your business, but you get it done, and let your breath out as you practically fall out of the portable bathroom. The door slams behind you and you jump, then pause a moment to catch your breath.

As you stand there, a blueish-white light catches your eye a little way away from you. At first it looks like a reflection in water; you can see it is a swamp behind the building, and you take three steps forward. That's when the light rises from the surface of the swamp and does a little dance in the air. It reminds you of a candle flame and it is beautiful and mesmerizing. You start to go closer and then suddenly remember your friends inside waiting for you.

If you investigate the light on your own, go to page 189
If you go back inside, go to page 86

"Yes," Josie answers for him. "Let's get out of here and let you catch your breath. We can come back if we need to."

Simon reluctantly agrees as he wobbles just a little on his feet. Josie takes him by the arm and leads him down the stairs. You are right behind them.

Once out of the stairwell, Simon shakes himself. Color has returned to his face. "Geez, that was insane," he says. "What was that?"

"It wasn't the druggie guy," Josie says, shaking her head. "It was something else. Sam says they call it 'Malebranche'."

"Like from *Dante's Inferno?*" Simon asks, his eyes wide and mouth agape.

Josie nods. "Sam says you are well-read. How did you know that?"

"I read it," he replies matter-of-factly. When Josie rolled her eyes, he went on. "They're a group of demons and their job is to keep corrupt politicians under the surface of a lake of boiling pitch."

"Ouch," Josie says.

"Yeah, not pleasant, but this one here, well, I guess he's gone rogue," Simon says, and chuckles.

"I don't find that very funny," Josie says.

"Does the Malebranche thing have anything to do with that thing downstairs?" you ask.

Josie nods. "So, I'll have to figure out how to take care of it later, for now, let's keep going."

You are all more than halfway down the hall when you realize you left the camera in the tower. "Wait for me!" you say and start back up the stairs to the tower, thinking only of not wanting to disappoint Jenna by not doing your job right. You see the camera on the small table in the corner at the far side of the tower room and head for it. You do not see the rope on the floor starting to slither towards your feet. And the rest happens so fast that you don't realize what is happening until the rope is winding around your head, suffocating you. Everything goes black.

By the time Josie and Simon come to look for you, it is too late.

THE END

"Since I've never done this before, I defer to you all to decide," you say.

Jenna shrugs. "Alright," she says, unclipping a walkie-talkie from her belt and holding it to her mouth. "Josie, Dave?"

"Go for Dave and Josie," Dave's voice comes back on the walkie.

"Can you guys come back to the equipment room? We're going to regroup," Jenna says.

"We'll be there as soon as we can," he replies.

While you wait, Jenna shows you how to use the various pieces of equipment again and demonstrates the night vision by handing you the camera, turning off the overhead light, and then stepping out into the darkened hallway. You move toward the doorway as she backs further into the darkness.

"So, you should be able to see me clearly," Jenna says, "and the walls, doors, etcetera. But for me, it's all pitch black."

"How does this capture ghosts?" you ask.

"A great question," Simon says.

"Well, night-vision is seeing things in the infra-red spectrum, and the theory is that we can capture energy manifestations that we cannot see with our human eyes," she says with a smile.

In the small screen of the viewfinder, you notice movement at the far end of the hallway behind Jenna. "Have you ever captured anything like a ghost on camera?"

"No," she replies, clearly disappointed at having to admit it. But then she perks right back up. "Not yet. I have a feeling this place will be different."

The movement behind her is getting closer. It is a large, shadowed form. Then you notice that there is another smaller shadowed form with it.

Jenna, oblivious, talks on. "I have really high hopes for this investigation, but how can I not? This is a huge place with so much history and activity reported."

You glance at Simon whose face is lit by the glow from the screen. He shakes his head and puts a finger to his lips, a smirk playing at the edges of his mouth, indicating for you not to say anything. You are torn between doing what he says and warning your new friend, but before you can decide either way, it's too late.

You watch as Dave comes into view, slinking up quietly behind Jenna. He emits a low growl, and you can see Jenna's eyes widen and her mouth drop open as she turns towards the sound. She starts to scream but also you see that she is taking a swing. Dave expertly catches the blow, grabs her around the waist, and hoists her in the air while she screams louder. You are about to panic when you realize they are both laughing.

He sets her back on her feet as she yells, "Dave! You are such a jerk!" But they are both still laughing.

"Alright, everyone in," Jenna says, ushering Dave and Josie into the room with you and Simon. "Awesome, now that I've had a proper heart attack thanks to my wonderful boyfriend, we can get this investigation going! We now have a full team and there is a lot going on here. I want us all to stick together for now, okay?"

Everyone nods.

"Alright, let's go!" Jenna leads the way with Dave right behind her. Josie and Simon follow, and you trail behind. But once you are out in the darkened hallway with them, you find you feel incredibly vulnerable being behind everyone. You glance over your shoulder, but you can't see anything but darkness. There is very little ambient light coming in through the dirty windows from streetlights outside. You have a flashlight in your hand that Jenna gave you and you turn it on. You shine it behind you and into the doorways gaping at you as you walk down the hallway.

"Everything okay back there?" Simon asks you over his shoulder.

"I think so," you say, but then you hear what sounds like heavy footsteps behind you. You stop and say, "Did anyone else hear that?"

They all stop walking and turn to you, shaking their heads. "No, what did you hear?" Jenna asks.

"I don't hear it now, but it sounded like footsteps behind me," you say.

Everyone stands, motionless, listening. You hear nothing.

"Hopefully your recorder caught it," Jenna says. "Let's keep going. Let us know if you hear it again."

You all continue down the hall. At the stairs, everyone pauses. Just then, there is a loud bang from somewhere.

"A door slamming?" Dave says.

"That's what it sounded like to me," Jenna says. "I think it came from upstairs."

"I thought it sounded like it came from the basement," Simon says.

"Hmm, which way should we go?" Jenna asks everyone.

To go upstairs, go to page 80
To go to the basement, go to page 115

You scream and start running. You pass Jenna, sprint up the stairs two at a time, hearing Jenna calling your name behind you, but you don't care. You are not stopping When you reach the top of the stairs you keep running toward the only light you see. It is the ambient light coming in through the main entrance to the building, and you burst through the doors into the cool night. You don't stop running until you reach the far side of the parking lot where one of the only working streetlights casts a pale-yellow light onto the street.

You are panting. You pull your phone from your pocket, but you have no signal. You look around. You think about starting to walk home until you reach a place where you have service, but you have no idea where you are. You look back at the horrible building and you see shadows moving through the door you left open, moving across the broken pavement of the parking lot, moving closer and closer to where you stand in the street light.

You don't know what to do, where to go. Your head starts to feel fuzzy, black spots dance in front of your eyes and then, everything goes black.

THE END

"No, we need to finish investigating up here," Simon replies. "I'm not going to give in to fear."

"Regardless, I think I'm pretty much done here. Whatever did that has left the room, and the addict guy is passed out," Josie says.

Simon frowns. "Is that possible?"

Josie shrugs. "In his mind it is."

"Okay, I guess we can keep going then," Simon replies. You are following them to the stairwell when Simon says over his shoulder, "Don't forget the camera."

"Oh! Thanks!" you say and turn back. You grab the camera and as you start once more for the stairs, you look through the camera's viewfinder and see the rope twitch and start to slither across the floor toward you. Without another thought, you give it a good, hard kick. The rope flies across the room, hits the wall on the other side, and falls to the floor in a spiritless heap. You hurry down the stairs to catch up with Josie and Simon just as they reach the hallway.

"Are Sam, Bobby, and Edward still with us?" you ask.

Josie nods. "And I'd really like to start moving things along. Can you call Jenna and see if they're finished what they're doing so we can regroup?"

"Sure," you say and unclip the walkie from your waist. "Come in, Jenna," you say into the walkie.

Jenna's voice comes back. "Go for Jenna."

"Josie is done her walk-through and would like to regroup. Are you done with setup?"

"All set. Let's meet in the equipment room," Jenna replies.

"On our way," you say.

But Josie and Simon stop again at the front of the hallway, both staring in through an open door. "Guys, what's going on?" you ask them.

"Look," Josie says. "This door was closed when we went by it before." Josie and Simon take several tentative steps towards the doorway, and you stay close, aiming the camera into the room over their shoulders.

"It's empty!" you say, surprised. Like most of the other rooms, there is nothing in the room except for bare bookshelves lining the walls.

"It wasn't empty earlier," Josie says with a frown. "He knows what I want to do, and he doesn't want to let me do it."

Simon asks the question you are also thinking. "Does that mean he is dangerous?"

Josie shrugs. "Scared people can be dangerous. Sam is afraid of him."

"Are you afraid of him?" you ask.

"I'm… cautious," is her reply. Simon sighs. Josie says, "Come on, let's go regroup downstairs so I can get everyone in this place cleared."

Jenna and Dave are already in the equipment room when you get there. Jenna holds out a platter of homemade chocolate chip cookies and Dave hands out bottles of water. You gratefully take a cookie.

Josie quickly swallows a cookie and chases it with almost a whole bottle of water, and then she proceeds to tell Jenna of all the energies she has so far encountered. "I need to start the clearing process now or I'm afraid I won't be able to, and bad things might happen."

"What kind of bad things?" Simon asks

"It doesn't matter. I need to get started," Josie insists.

"But I've had hardly any time to investigate!" Jenna laments. "Give me thirty more minutes, please?"

To keep investigating, go to page 94
To have Josie clear, go to page 76

But fear wins out in the end, and you put your phone away. It's for the best, you tell yourself, and do everything you can to ignore the heavy weight of guilt that is upsetting your dinner which is now churning in your stomach. You pick at your food until your parents are done and ready to go home. You can't wait to get home, crawl into bed, and forget about this day.

As you are leaving, you see a familiar face.

"Hey! What are you doing here?" Simon asks you.

"Having dinner with my parents," you reply.

"Ah, cool."

"You?" you ask, feeling awkward.

"I had met up with my girlfriend here for dinner. She had to get home. But just as we were finishing up, Jenna just texted me that she desperately needs backup on her investigation so I'm heading that way. I bet she'd be glad for your help, too. Want to come with me?"

Though you've only known Jenna and Josie for a couple weeks, you feel their influence over you as you think that maybe this is a sign that you shouldn't have bailed on the investigation. After all, if you weren't supposed to be there, you wouldn't have run into Simon like this, right?

If you decide to go with Simon, go to page 89
If you would rather go home, go to page 64

"I wish I could help, Simon, but I can't. Good luck," you say, and follow your parents out of the restaurant.

Once home, you continue to work on homework for a while, finally feeling like you are making headway in all your make-up work. It's late but you're not quite ready for bed, so you decide to take a long, hot shower. You have convinced yourself that you did the right thing, having argued with yourself that you shouldn't be forced into doing something you don't want to do just because you don't want to disappoint your friends.

"That's called 'peer pressure'!" you say aloud, ignoring the fact that they didn't pressure you, your own guilt did.

When you are in your room later, feeling good and relaxed, you find a text message on your phone from Jenna. It says: "Please we need your help! Desperate! Text if you can come!"

But you've already made up your mind. You put your phone on silent and go to bed.

In the morning, you have three more messages from Jenna from throughout the night, pleading for your help. You finally respond, saying, "Hi Jenna. Sorry that I didn't see your texts until now. I fell asleep early and didn't hear my phone. I hope it all went well. Text me all about it when you wake up."

However, as the day goes on, you don't hear from her. You try texting Josie with an apology but don't get a reply from her either. You assume they're just mad at you for bailing and not responding to Jenna's texts until you go into school Monday and find out that Josie, Jenna, Simon, and Dave have gone missing.

THE END

You blurt out, "I'll go with Josie." You surprise yourself, but you realize you are very curious to know what she does and how it works, and this is a perfect opportunity to witness it for yourself.

"Awesome! Okay, so take this camera. All you have to do is follow Josie and keep the camera on her. Feel free to ask her questions, but make sure they're not leading questions."

"What does that mean?" you ask, feeling a little silly for not knowing.

"A leading question is a question that is asked in a way that would put a suggestion in her mind of what the answer should be. Something like, 'Do you sense a little girl ghost in here?' is a leading question. Instead, you should ask something like, 'What do you sense in here?'. When she gives you information, a simple 'Tell me more,' is perfect. Does that make sense?"

You nod. "This ghost investigation thing is way more complicated than I realized," you say.

Jenna smiles. "That's because we're trying to do it right." She then turns to Josie. "Okay, are you ready?"

"Well, if you're not going to let me run screaming from this place, then yes, I suppose I'm ready," says Josie. She doesn't look like she is joking.

"Alright. Go wherever you feel pulled to go. We have full access to the building. Just watch where you're going. There's still some construction debris around and some sketchy flooring in places. And here," she hands you a walkie-talkie. "This place is big, so if you need us in a hurry, use that."

"Okay," you say to Jenna, clip the walkie to your waist, and then look at Josie. "Lead the way."

Josie clicks on a small flashlight, and you follow her out into a wide entryway and hallway.

"I can't believe how dark it is," you remark, looking around through the small screen of the video camera. Everything appears in various shades of green because of the night vision setting, but when you look up from the screen, you can only see Josie because of her flashlight. Just the slightest bit of ambient light is coming in through the front windows from whichever streetlights nearby are not broken.

"Yeah," Josie agrees half-heartedly, looks around the entryway, and then continues on down the hallway.

"Why did you say before that you wanted to run screaming out of here?"

"Sorry if I scared you," she says, stopping and turning to the camera. "I forgot you're new to this. That was more for Jenna. There's a ton of energy here, and it's making me cranky."

"Why is it making you cranky?"

Josie sighs. "Have you ever been somewhere, like a family party or something, where there's a whole bunch of people in the room, and they're all talking at once, and after a while, it gives you a headache?"

"Oh gosh, yes! It's the worst," you reply, nodding.

"Well, that's what I'm hearing, feeling, and seeing. All these people, talking at once. Some are talking to me, some are talking to themselves, some are fighting with others, some are just being jerks and making noise to make noise. I can't hear enough of anything to do anything about it."

"Are you talking about ghosts?" you ask.

"Well, yeah, you don't see any living people around here, do you?"

"No, sorry," you say.

"No, I'm sorry," Josie says. "Again, this energy, this noise is making me really cranky. I want to get rid of it as quickly as possible, but I can't because Jenna needs to investigate."

"So, what can we do?"

"Let's just keep walking. Eventually some of them will chill out or they'll get tired, and I can start to make sense of what's going on," she says, continuing down the hallway.

"Should I ask you questions? Or should I wait for you to start sorting things out?" you ask, eager to do your task in a way that will please Jenna and not annoy Josie.

"I'll start. So, I don't need to be a psychic to know that this building was once a factory of some sort. I think it was a place that made cloth or made something out of cloth. Some of these rooms along this hallway were storerooms, and I see piles and piles of bolts of cloth. There were offices down here too. I think those were at the front, and the storage rooms were on the back side."

In the tiny LED screen of the camera, you can see a staircase just ahead of Josie climbing up into darkness. She stops and when you get to her you can see that to the side of the stairs is a second set of stairs descending into a black hole to the basement.

A loud thud echoes from somewhere far away, and you strain your ears to figure out the direction it came from while your heart pounds hard in your chest.

"That sounded like it came from up there," Josie says, pointing up the stairs into darkness. "Let's follow the sounds."

To go upstairs, go to page 72

"I can't believe I'm saying this, but I guess I need to face my fear," you say. You take a deep breath in, nod, and add, "Lead on."

You follow Josie and Simon to the stairway. Simon motions for you to go ahead of him. "Just focus on putting one foot in front of the other. Don't think about what happened before or what might happen now," he says.

You nod and start up the stairs behind Josie. When your heart starts to pound hard from nerves, you focus on your feet as Simon suggested. It helps calm you, and you reach the tower without any incident. You look around, expecting to see something different, but it looks like it did when you and Jenna left earlier, the rope lying on the floor.

Simon walks over to the rope and kicks it with his foot. Nothing happens.

"Hey guys, want to try an experiment?" Josie says.

"What kind of experiment?" Simon asks with a frown.

"I'll try," you say before she can answer him. You feel braver now that you are in the tower, and nothing seems to be happening like before.

"Simon, just trust me," she says, tilting her head and batting her eyes at him. You can see him tense and then relax. "Both of you, come stand here next to me."

You do as she says, and Simon slowly moves to stand on her other side.

"Okay, now hold out your hands like this," Josie directs, holding her hands out straight in front of her. You and Simon both do the same. "What do you feel? Go with it for a minute or two before you answer."

You feel a bit ridiculous at first, standing there, all of you just holding your hands out into the air. But then you notice a tingle along your wrists and forearms, and then you feel something stronger.

"I feel something," you say, wondering how to put what you are experiencing into words.

"Just say it," Josie encourages you.

"Well, it's like… from my wrists almost to my elbows, it's a pleasant tingle, almost like if I had stuck my arms in a warm bath but… my hands…."

"I feel sick to my stomach," Simon says, and then takes a step backwards, dropping his hands. "Whatever my hands were feeling, it made me feel sick, but I agree that whatever energy my arms felt was pleasant."

"Yes," you say, "that's exactly it." You also step away.

Josie does as well. "Very good. Would you like to know what you were doing?"

"Of course," you and Simon reply simultaneously.

"So, I told you how before Dave's Spirit Guide had the drug addict guy in a kind of energetic hold?" she asks.

You and Simon both nod.

"It seems as if he's still in it," Josie says. "What I'm seeing is the man's form trapped within a thick, golden cube of energy. Your hands were feeling *him* and his unhealthy, angry, confused energy while your arms, from about wrist to elbow, were in the protective energy field."

"And he can't get out of it?" you ask.

"It appears not," Josie replies.

"That's a pretty neat trick," you say.

"I agree."

"Did you know that could be done?" Simon asks Josie.

She shakes her head. "I've never seen this before. It's new to me, but you can bet I'll be asking to do this with my own Spirit Guides."

"Does that mean Dave's Guide is still here?" you ask.

She shakes her head again. "It would seem that once he put the forcefield – for lack of a better term – in place, he was free to move about. He's probably keeping an eye on Dave."

"Wow," you say. "I'm so glad I stayed."

"Me, too," Josie says and gives you a smile.

"So, what now?" Simon asks. "Leave the guy?"

"I think I'll see if I can cross him over from inside there," she says. "This may be a very helpful technique for crossing over 'problem' ghosts."

"Should we check with Jenna first?" you ask.

"No, this guy is confused and angry, and now he's trapped. He's miserable. It's not fair to keep him here longer," she says.

"But he's a drug addicted jerk. What does it matter if he's miserable?" you say.

Josie looks at you. "Someone somewhere loved him at one time in his life. Someone cared whether he lived or died. Someone out there wished for him to be happy, healthy. He deserves peace just as much as anyone else."

You feel as though you have been slapped and you feel ashamed. "Sorry. You're right," you mumble.

"Alright, let me do this," she says, a little more gently.

To watch Josie help the ghost, go to page 104

You look at Josie through the camera viewfinder, perfectly framed in the doorway, the stairs fading into the darkness behind her. A shiver runs up your spine. "Um, should we be concerned that Bobby doesn't like whoever it is that is up there?" you ask.

Josie shrugs. "No more so than with anyone else here."

"So, not like with the stuff in the basement," you say.

"No, I… well…."

"Josie? Josie, if the guy up there has any ties to *that* stuff…," Simon starts.

"You're right," Josie says. "I am not sure. So, let's just tread very carefully," she says.

Simon sighs. "Okay."

"Okay," you say, less certain. You shiver again and say, "Whoa."

"What was that for?" Simon asks.

"I just got the strangest feeling of déjà vu," you say.

"Does that happen to you often?" Josie asks.

"No. I don't think so," you reply.

"Well, let us know if it happens again. Ready?" Josie says.

"Let's get this over with," you say, briefly questioning your own sanity.

To continue up to the tower, go to page 21

"The basement is the *last* place I would want to go, so let's go up," you reply with a nervous chuckle. *Neither option is very appealing*, you think, *especially if that loud bang did come from somewhere up there.*

"Alright," Josie says, and starts climbing the stairs.

You follow behind her. At the top of the stairs there is a wide landing with one set of double doors, and the stairs continue around and up to the third floor. Josie starts towards the doors and then stops and turns to the camera.

"Yeah, so... we're being followed," Josie says.

You turn and look behind you but see no one. "What do you mean?" you ask.

"There's a male spirit that I saw downstairs. He was the only one that wasn't making noise, and I could see him more clearly than most of the others. I wasn't sure about him, but he has followed us up here."

"Okay," you say. "Can you tell me more about him?"

Josie let out a long breath. "He's showing himself to me as a short man, but broad, like a bit chubby but not fat. He's wearing a dark brown three-piece suit, with a vest and all that. Even a hat. His face is really round and pock-marked all over. His nose is big and bumpy, too, like he's been in a lot of fights. His eyes are dark and squinty, and he has a cigar in his mouth. He looks unpleasant, but he's not threatening me. He's just watching us right now."

"And where are you seeing him?" you ask.

"He's standing about two feet to your right, near the railing," she replies.

You swing the camera around, your heart pounding with fear that you're going to see this man grinning at you on the little screen, but all you see is the railing and the stairs up to the third floor.

"Can you talk to him?" you ask, still very unsure how it all works and if it is even real.

"I am talking to him. Ghosts can hear my thoughts. But he's not talking to me. I'll make sure to tell you when anyone says anything so it can be on camera. Let's just keep walking around. He'll probably keep following us and eventually he'll talk to me. They always want to tell their stories."

"They do?"

Josie continues walking and goes through the double doors. "Yeah. I mean, think about it. You're stuck in the same place for years – decades or maybe even centuries – and no one can hear you. Wouldn't you want to talk to someone who could hear you?"

"I never thought about it like that," you say.

"That's really the only thing that keeps me going, doing this stuff for Jenna. I love her, but she's a maniac when it comes to this stuff. But these people that are trapped or stuck need help. And I get to help them. It's pretty cool. So, if I need to walk around in the dark being followed by a camera to help them, I'll deal with it."

"That's pretty amazing," you admit. "And it kind of makes it a little less scary when you put it that way."

"This stuff really isn't all that scary. Usually. I mean, sure, there are ghosts that want to scare you and cause trouble, but they're rare. Most of the time, we're the ones making this all scary. Sitting in the dark, waiting for something to happen... it's scary because we're at a disadvantage. Well, you are, because you can't see them, but they can see you. But as far as I can tell, they are far less powerful than most people give them credit for. Most of them, anyway. There are always exceptions," she says, and her eyes get a far-off look like she's remembering something.

You pan the camera around the room you're now in. It is mostly empty except for a few old and unidentifiable pieces of machinery and a few chairs scattered around. Thick wooden posts break the landscape here and there.

"This looks like one of the factory spaces," you say. "Sorry, was that leading?"

"It's okay, I was already thinking the same thing. There is a lot of residual energy here. I can see lots of big machines and people working around them," Josie says.

"What is 'residual energy'?"

"Oh, sorry. That's when energy is imprinted in a location, like a snapshot, or a clip from a movie that plays over and over again. I can't walk up to these people and start talking to them, because they're not really there, just like if someone watches a movie of you a hundred years from now, you're not really there," she replies.

"How can you tell the difference between a ghost or spirit and residual energy?" you ask, feeling like a journalist.

"Residual energy is much more static, and it's colder. I don't mean temperature, but more impersonal. It isn't an energy you can interact with, only observe. Whereas ghosts – and by ghosts, I mean a spirit who is stuck and haunting a location – have a warmer energy that has a higher charge to it that you can feel. Spirits, who are the ones who are not stuck, who've crossed over, have an even warmer, higher charge. A lot of people call it a 'vibration', but for some reason, I don't like that terminology."

Crossed over? Where do they cross over to? you wonder but decide to keep the question to yourself for now. Josie has come to the end of the large room, and there is another set of double doors. She goes through, into a hallway that has several closed doors, two of which are marked with the signs for men's and women's bathroom.

Josie points to the only open door which is at the end of the hallway. "That's where we need to go. There's someone standing in the doorway."

Your stomach clenches with fear. "Don't you think maybe we should check upstairs first?"

Josie shrugs. "We can if you really want to, but I think we should go there first."

If you insist on going up to the third floor, go to page 83
If you go into the room with Josie, go to page 113

"Jenna, I understand that this place is a paranormal gold mine, but I am afraid of what could happen to us if I don't clear it *now*," Josie says.

Jenna frowns, pauses, and then says, "Well, I know you well enough by now to know that if you are making that strong of a statement, I need to listen."

Josie let out a sigh of relief. "Thank you! Okay, let's head to the basement." She grabs another cookie and shoves it in her mouth as she heads back out into the darkened hallway, and everyone follows.

"It feels weird out here," Dave says.

"They know what's about to happen. Some are excited, some… not so much," Josie replies.

You have only gone a few more steps when an ear-splitting scream cuts through the air. Everyone stops in their tracks.

"What the—!" exclaims Jenna, hands covering her ears.

Before Josie or anyone else can respond, another scream cuts through the darkness, and then another and another. When the screaming finally stops, everyone pauses, waiting for whatever is next.

Then Josie says, "Ignore it. We have to keep going," and she hurries on.

As you reach the main doors about halfway down the hall, you hear a loud bang. Once more, you all stop. Then, all at once, the front door starts moving as though a giant is trying to break it down and all the doors off the hallway start opening and closing over and over.

"Keep going!" Josie yells over the noise and plows on down the hallway.

The doors stop their banging as you all reach the stairwell, where a thick black mist is forming, blocking the stairs. "It won't hurt you! Keep going!" Josie says over her shoulder as she walks straight through the strange vapor. Simon plunges through after her and the rest follow quickly but you are frozen on the spot. The mist is creeping closer to you, and it feels cold and damp on your skin. You shiver and take a deep breath, as though you are about to jump into a freezing cold lake.

To go to the basement, go to page 229

You take the camera from Simon's frozen hand and use the night vision and the viewfinder to find your way back to the door. You push at it, but it doesn't budge. You try the other one, and it won't open either.

"Arg! What am I going to do?" you yell, frustration moving you beyond fear. You go back to where Simon is, put the camera down, then take him by the arms and shake him as hard as you can. "Wake up!"

He stumbles and blinks several times, shaking his head. "Whoa, what happened?" he asks just as your flashlight flickers back to life in your pocket.

"I was just about to ask you the same thing," you say, picking up and handing him back the camera. "You were standing there like a statue for like ten minutes!"

"It was the weirdest thing – it was like I was having the most vivid dream of my life," Simon says. "I was here, in this room, but it was a working factory, and there were people everywhere. So weird!"

"Yes, I agree that the whole thing was very weird," you say. "Can we get out of this room now? I don't like it in here."

"Okay, let's head to the break room," he replies and starts toward the double doors on the far wall. You anticipate the doors not opening, but he pushes through with no issue, and you follow, taking one last look behind you.

Ahead of you is a short hallway with three doors on the left and two on the right. Simon stops walking suddenly when you both see a light in the last room on the right.

"Hello?" Simon calls out. "Who's there?"

A figure appears in the doorway, a flashlight in hand pointed at the two of you. "Oh, hey guys, I was wondering where you were!" Jenna says.

You and Simon look at each other, frowning. "Jenna? How did you get up here?"

She looks at you both in confusion. "What do you mean? And where were you guys?"

"We were in the big room," you say pointing to the doors you just came through.

"I just walked through there, and you guys were not there," Jenna replies, firmly.

"You could not have walked through there without seeing or hearing us," you say.

"What is going on here?" Simon asks.

"I don't know, but how about the three of us investigate the break room for a bit since we're all here," Jenna says.

To investigate the break room, go to page 176

Another, louder bang sounds then. "That definitely came from upstairs," Dave says, and everyone nods in agreement.

"Let's go!" Jenna declares and hurries up the stairs. At the top, everyone stops. Jenna takes several cautious steps towards the gaping black hole of the double doors leading into a large room. "Hello?" Jenna calls out. Everyone holds their breath, waiting for a response, but none comes. "Hello?" she yells, a bit louder.

Another loud bang sounds and everyone spins and looks up. "That came from above," you say, being closest to the stairwell.

"Come on!" Jenna says and is again hurrying up the stairs to the third floor. At the top, everyone again pauses. You look around and wonder why you are the only one panting. "Hello!" Jenna calls out. "Who is making those bangs? We just want to talk to you!"

Dave is the one who steps forward this time and shines his flashlight down the hallway. "Guys, I think I see some movement," he says.

Jenna goes to his side. "Where?" Dave points with his other arm. "Oh! I see it!"

Josie and Simon tentatively move to where they stand, and you follow.

"Watch the third doorway on the left," Dave says.

As you all stand there in a huddle, you see in the beam of Dave's flashlight the head and shoulders of a person as they lean out the doorway and appear to look in your direction.

"Oh my god!" you say quietly, your eyes widening.

"What's your name?" Jenna says, but the shadowed form disappears back inside the room. Jenna takes off at a run with

Dave right behind her. You follow, with Simon and Josie. By the time you get there, Jenna and Dave are inside the room.

"There's no one in here!" she says. "There's nowhere they could have gone! We just saw a shadow person! A ghost!"

There is another bang from down the hall. You turn and shine your flashlight in that direction and see a blur of a shadow move toward the stairwell. "It just went downstairs!"

Everyone takes off again, back down the hall, back down the stairs. Your foot catches on something and you stumble, but you manage to grab the railing to right yourself. Later, you will swear you heard a child laughing from somewhere nearby.

"I see it!" Jenna yells from ahead of you as she continues down the stairs, past the second-floor landing, back down to the first floor.

You skid to a halt behind Josie and Simon. Jenna and Dave are shining their flashlights down the hall toward the room Jenna called the equipment room. Now, everyone is breathing heavily as they stand, waiting for the shadow figure to show itself again. Your heart is pounding, though you are unsure if it is more from running or the anticipation.

And then you all see it, about halfway down the hall, the shadow runs from one side to the other. There is another loud bang and a sudden rush of air. You find the double front doors open wide to allow in the night. Jenna goes charging through the doorway to the outside with Dave right behind her. Simon follows as Josie says, "I don't know if this is a good idea!" But you both step outside and join the rest of the team on the broken front walkway, the cement cracked from years of weather.

The front doors slam shut behind you. You all turn to face the building. Dave and Jenna are shining their flashlights on the building. You can see several human shadow forms standing at the windows, looking out at you.

"They don't want us in there," Josie says.

Dave goes back to the doors and presses the handles, but the doors will not open.

"Let's check the side door," Jenna says and starts in that direction.

"You won't get in!" Josie says.

"But the rest of my stuff is in there!" Jenna replies.

"Trust me, Jenna. You can come back in the daylight to get it. They are not going to let us back in tonight," Josie says.

"Can't you cross them over?" Jenna says.

"Let's come back in the morning," Josie replies, "and we can take care of it all."

As Jenna stands there, scowling at her lack of options, you look up at the shadows watching from the looming brick structure. A shiver runs up your body.

"Anyone need a ride?" Simon asks.

"Yes!" you say, anxious to get away from this place.

THE END

"I think we should keep going up and then work our way down," you say, hoping she cannot hear the slight tremor in your voice.

But Josie sees through you. "I understand if you're afraid. This stuff is scary to any normal person. So, since this is your first investigation and you're just getting used to it all, I'll agree to keep going and we can come back here later."

"Thank you!" you say, relief flooding through you.

Josie turns and starts back down the hall toward the double doors, but then she stops abruptly in her tracks.

"What's going on? What's happening?" you ask as you stop next to her, the camera trained on her face.

She holds a hand up to signal silence, so you wait. After a few minutes of silence, she says, "It's the man from before. The one in the suit with the cigar. He wants to help us."

"What does that mean? How do you know we can trust him?" you ask.

"Good questions, let me see what he says," she replies. A few beats later, she says, "Well, he's saying that he knows every… *thing* here – that's how *he* put it – and can help us navigate it all. I guess some of them are… unusually difficult."

"And you believe him?" you ask. "You trust him?"

Josie pauses again for several beats and then sighs. "I do trust him. It's hard to explain. I feel like he's being truthful, like, I feel it in my gut, you know? And he's saying that he wants to help us for two reasons: one, because no one else has ever tried to do what we're doing, and he wants us to succeed so everyone can be at peace; and two, because he is trying to make up for some bad things he did in life."

Your eyes widen at that. "Like what?" you ask, but instantly regret it. You don't think you want to know.

"I think we'll find out more as we go," Josie replies.

You shrug. "Okay, is he saying anything else?"

"He introduced himself. His name is Sam Rossi," Josie says, nodding at the air where the specter supposedly stands.

"Nice to meet you, Sam," you offer, feeling a bit bad that you are skeptical of his motives.

"He says it's nice to meet you, too, and that it's okay if you are skeptical of him and his motives," she says, smirking at you when you look at her in shock. "He says he would be skeptical of him, too, if he were in our shoes."

"I don't know if that makes me feel any better about Sam," you reply, chuckling. "And I'm a little freaked out that he can hear my thoughts."

"You'll get used to it," Josie says.

"So… he can hear my thoughts and your thoughts, so presumably he can hear the thoughts of Jenna and Dave, too. And you can hear him in your mind, so it's kind of like you can hear his thoughts. Is that right?" you ask.

"Yes," she replies.

"So how come I can't hear him?" you ask.

"Great question," Josie says. "Our thoughts are essentially energy forms. Ghosts are energy forms, so I think that makes it easier for them to hear our thoughts, but in general, living humans aren't able to receive these energy forms as clearly as I do, as all Mediums do. It's part of the 'gift' – I hate that word, by the way. I prefer 'ability'. But you and other living humans do receive intuitive information. It's that 'gut feeling' you get that something is wrong and then you find out someone died or knowing that your favorite cousin is going to call you before your phone rings. It's just not as clear for you where the information is coming from."

"Oh. Well… that makes so much sense," you say, bowled over by what she just said. But you collect yourself, remembering that you have a job to do. "Okay, well, so where should we go next?"

To keep going, go to page 16

You remember Jenna saying she didn't want anyone investigating on their own, so despite your deep curiosity, you hurry back inside.

"I saw a light in the swamp!" you tell them as soon as you get through the door. All four heads snap in your direction.

"What do you mean?" Jenna asks.

"I came out of the port-a-potty and there was this light floating out in the swamp! Like a little flame!" you tell her.

"Like a will-o'-the-wisp!" she says.

"What's that?" Dave asks.

"It's from folklore and tells of a light that mimics a lantern or candle, and is said to lure people to their doom," she says.

"I'm glad I didn't follow it," you say. "But I was tempted."

"Those things are just swamp gas," Simon says.

"My brother, ever the skeptic," says Jenna.

Simon lets out a sigh of frustration. "Jenna, you know I will always offer a scientific explanation where I can."

"Yes," she says, "but we won't conclude that without investigating it. Fair?"

"Fair," Simon agrees.

"Okay, first, let's all go out and see if we can see this light," she says.

Everyone files outside.

"Show us where you were standing when you saw it," Jenna says to you.

You walk to the edge of the swamp at the far side of the parking lot, behind the port-a-potty. "I was here, and the light hovered and kinda wiggled, right out there, but I don't see it now," you say, disappointed.

You all scan the swamp for any signs of a light, but after a few minutes, Simon says, "I don't see anything."

"Well, let's go inside. We can come back out later if we have time," Jenna says. Once inside, she says, "Okay, is everyone good? Enough water, snacks, and bathroom time?"

Everyone nods.

"Great! Let's investigate!"

If you investigate with Jenna and Dave, go to page 221
If you investigate with Simon and Josie, go to page 109

"Let's just finish up here before we go upstairs," you say.

"Sounds like a plan," Josie says. "Simon?"

"Yeah, whatever works for you guys," he says.

Josie continues to walk down the hall. Again, she zigzags from one open doorway to another as she goes.

"Anything?" you ask after extended silence.

Josie shakes her head. "Nothing. All seems quiet down this end of the hall."

"Alright, so, what do we do?" you ask.

"Let's just go up to the tower," she says and starts back down the hall.

When she is near the entrance to the tower stairs, you say, "Should we be concerned that Bobby doesn't like whoever is up there?"

Josie shrugs. "I don't think so."

"So, it's not like the stuff in the basement," you say.

"No, I… well…."

"Josie? Josie, if the guy up there has any ties to *that* stuff…," Simon starts.

"You're right," Josie says. "I am not sure. So, let's just tread very carefully," she says.

Simon sighs. "Okay."

"Okay," you say, less certain.

"Ready?" Josie says.

You look at her through the camera viewfinder, perfectly framed in the doorway, the stairs fading into the darkness behind her. A shiver runs up your spine. "Let's go," you say, briefly questioning your own sanity.

To go up to the tower, go to page 21

You decide to put your fears aside once and for all. "Sure, but let me check with my parents," you say. They are waiting by the entrance of the restaurant. You explain the situation and plead with them, telling them that your new friendships depend on it. They reluctantly agree to let you go with Simon.

"Okay, let's go," you say to him.

As he drives off, your heartbeat quickens with nerves. You shift in the seat, tugging at the seatbelt, unable to settle.

It seems he can sense your nervousness when he says, "Is this your first time investigating?"

"Yes," you admit.

"You shouldn't be afraid. The only thing you have to fear is boredom most of the time. These things are a lot of sitting around and waiting. Waiting for something to happen, and most of the time nothing happens."

"Really?" you ask.

"Really," he replies.

"How many investigations have you been on?"

"Oh, I'd say about a dozen, unofficially," he says with a grin. When you look at him quizzically, he says, "Not all of them were planned."

"And they're not scary?"

"Not really."

"But you believe in this stuff, right? Ghosts and things?"

"Well...."

You look at him in surprise. "You don't?" You're not sure why, but that makes you feel a lot better.

"Let me just say that I have witnessed plenty of things I can't explain, but I'm not sure ghosts are... well, what we think they are."

"Fair enough," you reply.

"We're almost there," he says, pointing to his GPS display. You look out the window but all you see is darkness and trees.

"Where the heck are we?" you ask.

"This area used to be an industrial park, but the owner went bankrupt, and all the buildings ended up abandoned. I think most of them have been torn down except for the one we're going to because it has some historical significance and the historical society has fought to keep it standing," he says, and you are impressed by his knowledge.

He turns into a wide parking lot. The badly broken pavement has large potholes and weeds growing up through the cracks leading to a four-story towering brick monster with dozens of black eyes that seem to be staring into your soul.

"This place is spooky," you say as you get out of the car.

"Most places can seem spooky in the dark," he says. You both walk towards the building.

"I have a feeling this place would look spooky in bright sunlight, too," you say, and shiver.

"I guess it depends on what spooks you," he says very nonchalantly.

"Okay, can you tell me again that I shouldn't be afraid?"

Simon chuckles. "You really have nothing to be afraid of. We've all done this before, and we know how to keep everyone safe. The most important thing to remember is to watch where you step. The most dangerous thing about investigating is knocking your shins on something while you walk around in the dark."

You laugh, feeling your fear ease just a little. You follow Simon to a door at the side of the building that enters into a small, dimly lit room.

"Jenna!" Simon calls out.

"Coming!" Her voice echoes from somewhere not too far away, and then a flashlight beam breaks the darkness just beyond the room, barely visible through a doorway opposite from where you're standing.

When she appears in the room and shines her flashlight on Simon, he says, "And I brought more reinforcements," and points to you.

"You came back!" she says, bouncing over and enveloping you in a hug.

"Yeah, I was at dinner with my parents, and I ran into Simon. He said you needed help, so here I am," you say to her, warmed by her greeting.

"Oh, I'm so glad! This place is crazy! But I don't want to tell you too much yet. I left Dave and Josie down in the basement. But I think you guys should start where we started. You can either go up to the tower room on the fourth floor or you can go to the second-floor break room," she says with a knowing smile.

You look at Simon and he says to you, "Okay, what do you think?"

If you go to the tower, go to page 136
If you go to the break room, go to page 8

Josie starts down the stairs as fast as she can go and you are hot on her heels, not wanting to be left behind with whatever spooked her. You make it past the second floor and the first floor is in your sight when you hear Jenna's voice.

"Hey, guys! What's going on?" she asks, shining her light on you. You go momentarily blind for a second, and in that moment, you feel your right foot catch on something, as though a hand grabbed at your ankle to prevent you from moving forward. You feel yourself start to lurch forward, your arms flail, hoping to catch a railing, but there is nothing but air all around you until your body slams against the stairs. You tumble and roll down the rest of the way to the floor where you lay sprawled, one of your legs bent at an awkward angle.

You are then suddenly looking down at your own body. "What the heck?" you say.

Jenna is crouched at your side with Dave standing over her while Josie is sobbing in Simon's arms saying, "It's so awful! No, no, no! I can't… this place is too much!" And as you watch, the form of a little boy, shimmering like an oil spill in the summer, smiles and waves at you as he steps into your lifeless body on the floor. Your body jerks and takes a gasping breath before crying out in pain at your broken leg.

"What is happening?" you say, but no one hears you.

"Guys, I'm getting Josie out of here, and I'm calling nine-one-one," Simon says as he leads Josie away from the gruesome scene.

You then realize Josie should be able to hear you. "Jo—!" is all you manage before a hand is wrapped around your mouth.

"Sorry, but this is how it has to be," a gravelly voice says in your ear. Your eyes widen in fear as you are turned to face whoever has you in their grasp and see who you assume is the man that had been following you and Josie. She had described him as a short broad man wearing a dark brown three-piece suit, with a vest and a hat. She said his face was round and pock-marked all over with a big and bumpy nose, dark and squinty eyes, and with a cigar in his mouth. He smiles past the cigar. "Sam's my name."

Before you can do anything else, you are enveloped by a bright, white light.

THE END

"Fifteen minutes," Josie bargains.

"Twenty!" Jenna counters.

"Ugh, fine, but not a second more," Josie relents, and you see Simon take a step closer to her. "I am going to start outside by the swamp while you finish up in here."

"Can I stay with you, Josie?" you ask. "I'd like to see you through the whole process."

"Sure," she replies with a nod and a small smile. She turns and goes out the door you had come in through earlier in the night, a time which feels like a lifetime ago to you now. You step outside behind her and Simon follows. You give him a nod. It feels like you are both Josie's most reliable guardians.

Josie moves along the edge of the parking lot to the grassy area that extends several feet down to the edge of the swamp. It is a nice night out, and you are glad to be outside, but as you all move closer to the swamp, you shiver.

"There is a lot of energy here in the swamp," Josie says. She is standing with her toes nearly at the water's edge. She closes her eyes and holds out her hands, palms facing forward, arms straight. You keep the camera on her at an angle and can see she is taking big, deep breaths. You want to know what she is doing but are afraid you might break her concentration.

It's Simon who breaks the silence. "Uhm… what is that?" he says. He is pointing out into the swamp so you look up from the viewfinder, and you can't miss it. Far out into the swamp, hovering in the air about four feet off the surface, is a glowing orb of bluish-white light. Then, another one rises up out of the swamp near the first, and then another and another. As you and Simon stand there watching, dozens more rise from the murky waters of the swamp to join the others, and then, they start to slowly float toward you.

"Um… Josie?" you say with apprehension.

"It's okay," she says, finally opening her eyes. "They're souls, and they're ready to move on."

The glowing orbs, each about the size of a basketball, drift closer and closer, and just before they reach Josie, they whiz upwards into the sky. It takes only a few minutes, and they are all gone.

"Wow!" you breathe.

"Right?" Josie says with a smile. "*That* is why I put up with all this other stuff," she says, waving her arm at the beast that is the building before her.

"That was incredible," you say.

"Josie is incredible," Simon says quietly.

She smiles at him, and you can practically feel the electricity passing between them.

"Well, I think Jenna's time is up," Josie says, breaking the spell between her and Simon. "Let's get back inside so I can finish this up. I can't wait to get away from this place."

As you all go back inside the equipment room, Josie takes the walkie from you and presses the button. "Jenna, I'm done outside and I'm starting in here whether you're ready or not."

Jenna's voice comes back over the walkie, clearly disappointed. "Oh, okay. Do you need us there for the clearing?"

Josie replies cryptically, "Yes, I think you *want* to be present for this one."

"On our way," Jenna replies.

Josie grabs a cookie from the open container on the table and disappears through the dark doorway, back into the hall. You and Simon follow.

"Feels weird out here," he says.

"They know what's about to happen. Some are excited, some… are not so much," Josie replies.

As you reach the stairs, you see Jenna and Dave coming down from the second floor. "I would kill to investigate this place for a week!" Jenna says, then quickly adds, "But I understand why you want to move everything on."

"I appreciate that," says Josie. "Okay, let's get downstairs and get this over with!"

To go to the basement, go to page 229

"I'm going to run and set up the cameras fast and then we'll come down, okay?" Jenna says.

Josie shrugs. "Do whatever you need to do," and she continues down the stairs.

You can feel the electricity pass between Josie and Simon as they pass each other on the stairs. Once they have gone further up and you and Josie have started down the basement steps, you say, "Is it okay that they're not coming with us?"

Josie shrugs again. "We'll find out."

"It is darker than dark down here!" you say as you step off of the bottom stair and onto the cement floor. It is cool and a little musty.

"It's like the darkness is swallowing the light from my flashlight," Josie says.

"That sounds like the first line of a horror novel," you say with a nervous chuckle. "But you're right. Even the greens of the night vision look duller than they did upstairs."

"I don't like it down here. I think it has to do with the swamp out back," Josie says.

"There's a swamp out back?" you say.

"Didn't you see it when we pulled in?" she says.

You feel a little foolish. "No, I didn't. I think I was too focused on this enormous and frightening building."

"I get that," she says. She moves slowly through the wide-open expanse of space broken only occasionally by a thick cement post.

You examine one through your camera screen. "Is this all that's holding up this whole place?" you marvel.

"Unbelievable, isn't it?" Josie responds. You can tell from her voice that she's moved further away from you, and when you pan the camera, you cannot find her. You can't even find the beam of her flashlight. "Josie? Where did you go?"

"I'm right here!" she says, but she sounds far away. You move in the direction you think her voice came from, and then suddenly there she is, right in front of you and you almost bump into her.

"Whoa!" she says. "What the heck was that all about?"

"I couldn't see you! Or your light!" you say.

"But I was right here!" she says.

"Is Sam still with us?" you ask.

"Yes," she replies. "Give me a minute."

Standing there in the dark, not knowing what just happened, seconds feel like an eternity. You want Josie to hurry up. Finally, she says, "Okay, first…," she grabs your arm and gently guides you about three feet to your right. "Alright. So, apparently, we were just standing in some sort of weird concentration of energy. It's why Sam wanted us to come down here, but we have to be really careful."

"Why?" you ask.

"Because—"

BANG! Across the room something crashes and there is a sudden rush of air. You can see a faint rectangle of light – or rather, less dark darkness – coming in through what you assume is a doorway that has just opened.

"What was that?" you ask anyway.

"Come on, let's find out," she says. But she continues to grip your arm as you both walk toward the doorway, as though she is unwilling to be too far from you. You aren't afraid to admit you are relieved that she seems frightened too.

"It's a bulkhead," you say, when it comes into view in your camera screen. There is a short set of cement stairs leading up to the outside world. The inner door has been blown open, and there is a breeze coming in. The night outside is less dark than the basement, and you feel pulled to be out there where it is probably safer.

"Let's go outside and look around," Josie says, and again you feel relieved that she is on the same page as you.

You let her go up the stairs first and follow close behind while she continually glances back to make sure you are there. You step out onto the grass and immediately the stink of the swamp hits you.

"I wonder why these were open," you say, gesturing to the wide-open double doors traditional to a bulkhead.

"Maybe it was the construction workers who left them open," she says.

You frown. "How did you know there have been construction workers here?"

"Sam told me," Josie replies. "I guess he and Bobby and some of the other ghosts sometimes like to play pranks on them, moving their tools around, hiding things, making weird sounds, and—"

BANG!

Again, something slams. You look down into the bulkhead to see the same door that had blown open is now shut. You hurry down the short flight of stairs and try to open the door, but it will not budge.

"I do not like this. At all," Josie says. "Let's head around to the side of the building and go in through the equipment room. Try giving Jenna a call on the walkie as we go."

You follow Josie along the back wall of the building and press the walkie, but nothing happens. "I think it's dead," you say, shivering at the term.

"Okay, well I know where Jenna keeps the spare batteries," she says just as she rounds the corner of the building. She tugs on the door for the equipment room, but like the other door, it will not budge.

Just then, Jenna, Dave, and Simon come walking around the front corner of the building. "Hey! What are you guys doing out here?" she says.

"We were in the basement," Josie says, then recaps quickly what you both had just experienced.

"What the heck?" Jenna replies. "We were on our way down to you, and when we reached the first floor, the front door burst open. We went to investigate, stepped outside, and the door slammed shut and wouldn't open!"

"Someone doesn't want us in that building," Dave says.

"But who?" Jenna asks. "Josie, any ideas?"

"Honestly, there is so much happening in there, I'm not sure it's any one ghost, entity, energy…. I think they're all working together," Josie says.

"What does Sam think?" you ask.

"Who is Sam?" Jenna asks.

Josie shrugs. "He was still in the basement when the door slammed," she tells you.

"Can't you still talk to him? Mind to mind?" you ask.

Josie shakes her head. "I can't hear anything or anyone from out here. It's like there's a barrier around the place."

"Maybe we should go," Simon says.

"But my equipment!" Jenna exclaims. "And the investigation has hardly begun!"

"Jenna, I think he's right," Josie says. "I have a feeling that whatever is happening in that building is beyond us."

"But my stuff!" Jenna says again.

Dave steps forward and puts a hand on Jenna's shoulder. "We can come back in the daylight. Maybe whatever is keeping us out will let us in then."

After a lot more back and forth, Jenna very reluctantly agrees to leave, but only after each door is checked again.

* * * * *

The following Friday you are at Jenna's house. Dave, Josie, and Simon are there. They were not able to get back into the building until the day before when Dave's mother's friend went with them.

"And there is nothing on any of the equipment!" Jenna exclaims. "Every recorder, every camera, it's nothing but blackness and static."

"Sorry, Babe," Dave says.

"I'm sorry, too, Jenna," says Simon. "I know how much this investigation meant to you."

"Me too," Josie says.

"Same for me," you say. "My first experience investigating, and it was insane! It's too bad there's no evidence."

"I appreciate all you guys," Jenna says. "I'm willing to admit that this place beat me."

"That's big of you, Jenna," Simon says.

"But I'm not going to let that stop me," she says with a grin, looking at each of you. "So, who's ready for our next investigation?"

THE END

"Jenna!" you finally yell in a strangled panic.

"Stand your ground!" she yells back. "They feed off fear!"

But you have never felt fear like this in your life. The ashen, transparent face of the man who screamed at you is so close you can see that his sunken eyes are bloodshot. And then you realize that it was just a head, floating like a balloon.

And that makes you chuckle. Suddenly, you're not as afraid. The chuckle turns into another chuckle and then a full-blown laugh. The man frowns at you and disappears in a blink.

You are still laughing when Jenna rushes over to you. "Did you get it on camera?" she asks.

You shake your head as your laughter subsides. "I was trying to turn it on when I saw him."

"Shoot. Okay, well, hopefully we caught it on audio," she says and pushes the button on the camera to start recording. "I'm going to leave an extra audio recorder here, too."

"Did you see him?" you ask her.

"No," she replies, shaking her head. Her curly red hair is in a ponytail that swings back and forth. "But I heard him. This place is crazy already! We haven't even started the investigation!"

Jenna pulls another camera from the bag and turns it on.

"What's next?" you ask.

"I don't have enough equipment to put a camera in every place I would like, so…. Let's see, two down here, because this is the one place where there was a definite sighting of an apparition – now by two people! One is with Dave and Josie, and we have this one. Okay, I have one more camera up in the equipment room. Let's go grab it and head to the tower."

You follow Jenna back upstairs, expecting the ghost man to jump out at you any second. But you make it back to the room where Jenna grabs the last bag and heads back into the hallway. You follow her back to the staircase and this time start to climb up.

To go to tower, go to page 128

"But you'll have to do it all aloud," Simon tells Josie, "so we can get it on video and audio for Jenna."

"Right," Josie says.

You take a few steps back and lean against a wall at the far side of the tower, out of the way but where you can watch whatever Josie is about to do.

"Okay, Corey, it's time to have a chat," she says. It looks like she is talking to the air, but she is aiming her words at that space where you and Simon both felt the weird energetic tingling. "He's glaring at me," Josie says over her shoulder to Simon and the camera. "Corey, if you don't talk to me, you're going to stay stuck in that box for the rest of eternity. That doesn't sound like much fun, does it?"

Silence hangs in the air but you swear you hear something like a static-electricity crackle.

"He just shook his head," Josie says quietly. "Okay, Corey. Do you understand that you died?... He just shrugged. You overdosed on drugs, Corey. But you did it, I think, to quiet the voices you were hearing, the voices you *thought* were in your head. Is that right?... He's looking at me with shock, and then he nodded. Corey, it wasn't drugs making you hear voices, it was your choice of a hide-out. This building is haunted by ghosts, and some of those ghosts were messing with you, teasing you, just like you were doing to all of us earlier. Do you understand what I'm telling you?"

There is a stretch of silence that Simon finally breaks. "What's happening?"

Josie holds her hand up to silence him. Moments beat on along with your heart drumming in your chest. You think you hear more crackling in the air and wonder if it is your imagination.

Finally, Josie turns towards the camera and says, "He's shocked by what I said. He died in a drug-induced stupor and just thought he was on a weird high, doing the things he was doing. He's sad, too, for the life he lost." She turns back toward where Corey supposedly stands trapped and says, "What kind of life did you want? What did you want to be when you grew up?"

More silence, more static crackles in the air. Many minutes pass while Josie listens.

"He said that he always wanted to be a dad. He wanted to get a job in computers, get married, and be a dad so he could play catch and teach his kids how to work on cars like he did with his dad. But it was after the sudden death of his own dad that he first tried drugs with some kids he didn't normally hang out with, and the rest is… history."

"That is sad," Simon says. "One bad choice set his life on a very different track than what it might have been."

"I'm sorry it happened to him," you say. "I'm sorry I was so quick to judge."

"And he's sorry for the problems he caused earlier," Josie says. "He's eager to go. He doesn't want to stay here any longer. My guide is here, Mother Elk Spirit, and she has brought his father with her…. The energy field is dissipating…. He's hugging his father… and he's… gone…."

"So, he's *gone* gone?" you ask.

Josie shrugs. "He's gone on to somewhere else. Wherever it is that we belong when we die."

"Wow. That was amazing," you say.

"Isn't she?" Simon says, beaming at her.

"They're not always that easy," Josie says, trying to ignore the flush that has risen to her cheeks at Simon's words. "Some don't want to go. Some don't want to listen."

"Well, I'm impressed, easy or not," you say. "I just wish I could actually *see* it all happening."

"Now you sound like Jenna," Josie chuckles.

"What now?" Simon says.

"Let's work our way down. There's nothing left to do up here," she says.

As he heads down the stairs, Simon pulls the walkie talkie from his belt and presses the button. "Jenna, we're done in the tower and heading to look around on the fourth floor."

"Got it," Jenna's voice returns. "We're still up on the second floor, in the break room."

"Okay," Simon replies and reclips the walkie to his belt.

In the hallway, Josie looks left and then right, then left again, and then back to the right. You guess she is trying to sense which way to go, which way the spirits are. She starts to walk to the right, back toward the main stairs.

But you have only gone a few steps when someone comes walking out of one of the side rooms and rushes across the hall, through the open doorway of another room.

"Did you guys see that?" you ask. "Who was that?"

You all stop walking.

"No one else should be up here," Simon says. Then he calls out, "Hello? Who's there?"

"That looked like a living person," you say.

Simon takes a cautious step towards the room the person went into and looks over his shoulder. "Josie? Any idea on who or what that was?"

Josie shrugs. "It happened so fast but… I don't think it was a living person."

"It sure looked like one," you say.

Simon takes a few more steps to the doorway and peers in, shining his light around and panning the camera. "There's no one in here," he says, shaking his head. "I would have sworn that was a flesh-and-blood person."

"Me too," you say. You step into the room behind Simon. It is just a square space with a door on one side and one window on the other. A few pieces of discarded wood are propped in one corner, but the room is otherwise empty.

You turn back to the doorway where Josie lingers, staring at the floor with a frown. "Josie? Are you okay?" you ask.

"Yeah," she replies, without looking at you. "Just trying to figure out what I'm sensing."

You and Simon wait in the silence and the dark for her to continue, but then the clattering of a piece of wood as it falls and slides across the floor startles all of you.

"Simon, did you do that?" Josie asks.

"I'm nowhere near the wood!" he replies as all three of you train your flashlights on the corner where three other two-by-fours are leaning and then at the spot in the middle of the room where the rogue piece has landed.

"Do you think you got it on camera?" Josie asks.

"It's possible I was aiming it in that direction," he says. "Did the guy we saw do that?"

"I'm not sure," Josie says. "I want to go downstairs to the third floor and check out the room below this one."

"Can you tell us why?" Simon asks.

"Not yet," she replies.

"Alright, let's head down there," Simon replies, leading the way out of the room. But before you all reach the stairs, your attention is drawn to the one door in that hallway that is closed.

"Shouldn't we try to get into that room first? I mean, since we're up here," you say.

If you all decide to try to open the door, go to page 132
If you decide to go on to 3ʳᵈ floor, go to page 195

Jenna looks at you and says, "Why don't you go with Josie and Simon for now. Head on up to the tower, and Dave and I will go to the second-floor break room," Jenna says.

"Sounds like a plan," Josie says. She looks at Simon, and you see a little twinkle in her eyes. "Ready, Simon?"

"Let's go," he replies to her with a smile, though you sense a thread of nervous excitement in him.

"Ready?" she asks you.

"Ready!" you respond.

Josie heads out the door and you follow with Simon behind you. You feel a thrill of nervous excitement at getting back into the investigation with a real Medium. You have so many questions for her, but you start with, "Hey Josie, can you tell me a bit about Spirit Guides now?"

"Sure," she says. "Spirit Guides are spirits that have crossed over – not stuck spirits like the ghosts we have here – and they are with us to guide us in different aspects of our lives. They are the nudge to take our lives in a certain direction, or the 'gut feeling' you probably have had at some point. Does that make sense?"

She starts climbing the stairs.

"Yeah, I think I get it. So, does that mean you see the ghosts of dead people and Spirit Guides, too?" you ask.

"Actually, I only see Spirit Guides when they want me to see them, like when they need my help to pass on a message," she says, reaching the second-floor landing and continuing up.

"Oh, that's interesting," you reply, but you are huffing and puffing while Josie and Simon do not seem fazed by the exertion, and you fall behind them on the stairs. "And you said… earlier that… one of… Dave's guides… helped you?"

"Yeah, it's actually pretty interesting. Dave's pretty protective – of Jenna, of course – but of me, too, and even Simon. His guide is this big man, as wide as he is tall with long dark hair and a big, bushy dark beard. And he shows himself wearing a big fur coat, like bear skin or something. He got very protective of me earlier when the guy in the tower misbehaved."

"How so?" Simon asks, and you are relieved since you are out of breath as you reach the fourth-floor landing.

"It was pretty cool. It was like he put some sort of energetic binding on the guy so he couldn't move," Josie says as she heads down the hall.

"Should we be concerned?" you ask.

Josie just shrugs. "I'm sure we will be okay."

Simon glances over his shoulder at you and you exchange a doubtful look with each other, but you both continue on after Josie. When her flashlight lights up the doorway to the tower stairs, your heart starts to race. You freeze. You feel like you have ice in your veins and your feet feel like they are stuck to the floor.

Simon and Josie only notice when they reach the door and turn back to you. Simon frowns and asks, "Are you okay?"

You shake your head. "How do you guys do this?"

"Do what?" Josie asks.

"Do *this!* Ghost hunting! Going into these weird and terrifying situations again and again," you say.

"It's really not that scary once you get used to it," Josie says.

"Are you serious? You were harassed by a dead guy up there! And did Jenna tell you what happened to us?" you reply.

"Um… no, she didn't," Josie says, her frown matching Simon's. "What happened?"

"Oh, only that she almost got choked out by the noose up there that I had to pry from around her throat and body, and I *also* got groped and harassed," you tell them.

"Seriously?" Simon asks.

"I wouldn't make up something like that," you reply.

"That's not what I meant. Sorry. It's just that… that's big," he says.

"Yeah. It is. So yes, I'm a bit scared to go back up there. I'm sorry," you say, your face suddenly burning with embarrassment at admitting you are a coward.

Josie and Simon walk to where you stand frozen, though it seems that the admission has freed your feet, at least.

"You have every reason to be frightened," Josie says. "I'm sorry we didn't take you into consideration. Honestly, I forgot that this is your first time doing this."

"Me too," Simon adds. "But Josie was right when she said that it's not that scary once you get used to it. It takes time, but working with Josie, who has insight into the people doing these things, helps you to understand that these are just that: people. People who are often frightened or confused."

"And sometimes they're just lonely, and they lash out. Think about it. These people here, some of them don't understand that they're even dead. Years and years pass, and they don't see other people. Then suddenly, there are people here," Josie says.

"I never thought of it like that. When you put it that way…," you say.

"Not so scary, huh?" Simon finishes for you.

You nod.

"Okay, so, do you feel ready to face your fear and go up to the tower?" Josie asks.

If you decide investigating isn't for you, go to page 45
If you decide to face your fear, go to page 68

You shake your head reluctantly. "Jenna said for you to go where you're pulled, so let's go in there," you say.

"Okay," says Josie.

She turns and walks into the room, and you follow close behind. Immediately you feel dizzy and sick to your stomach.

"Wow, I don't feel very good," you say.

"Yeah, the air is thick. What you're feeling is a lot of bad energy. There's a very unhappy female ghost with us, along with a lot of memories of bad things that happened in this room," Josie says.

"Wow... okay, can you describe the female ghost for me? Where is she and what does she look like?"

"She's pacing back and forth along the room," says Josie, gesturing with her arm to indicate the length of the rectangle-shaped room. As you pan the camera, you see a long counter with cabinets above and below lining the back wall, a double sink half-way along and, at the far end in the corner, stands an old refrigerator. A shiver runs up your spine.

"I can see her, but I'm also seeing residual energy of the things she did here," says Josie.

"What did she do?"

"As best I can tell, she was like a 'Black Widow' - preying on the men that worked here. She would cook them meals and charm them with compliments to get them to do stuff for her, which is amazing because she's not very attractive. She's short and very stout with a face that looks like a mole – beady eyes, pointy nose, small, protruding mouth. But it would seem she was good at charming and manipulating the men. I'm pretty sure she killed at least a half-dozen of them."

"She's a murderer?" you ask, amazed.

"Yup, and she's not happy with me for saying she looks like a mole," said Josie with a chuckle.

"What's her name? Will she tell you?"

Josie is silent for a minute. "She won't tell me but... ah, there's someone else here now. I think it's one of her victims. Her first victim? He says her name is Ellie Watson, and he admits that she isn't very pretty but that she could be very sweet when she wanted to be, and to a lonely man, that was attractive. He's angry with himself for allowing her to manipulate him, for getting himself killed."

"Is this the same man that was following us earlier?" you ask.

"No," she shakes her head. "This guy is taller and thinner, and dressed more like a laborer. The other guy looked more like he was the guy who runs the show. This guy looks like one of the workers."

"That's so sad," you say.

"He is sad. He looks like a beaten man, so you might be feeling his sadness. But Ellie is getting mad that we're talking about her."

Just then, one of the upper cabinets pops open and a plate goes flying across the room and shatters against the wall.

If you scream and run from the room, go to page 124
If you are excited by what happened, go to page 18

Before anyone can reply, you hear footsteps again. They are heavy and sound like they are moving fast in your direction. The others all turn toward the hallway, also hearing the footfalls.

Then, a large, shadowed form comes out of the darkness and rushes by. You feel the breeze as they go, and you hear the steps as they run down into the basement.

"Who was that?" Dave asks.

"Was that an actual person?" Simon asks.

"Hey, you can't be here!" Dave yells down the stairs and then starts down after the shadow.

"Dave, no!" Jenna yells but he doesn't stop, and she starts down after him. Josie and Simon follow, leaving you to hesitate for only a second before you also follow.

"It was a person!" Dave is saying when you reach the basement. "There!" He is pointing to the other side of the large space where a rectangle of light can be seen coming through a doorway. A shadow in the shape of a person moves in front of the light and then goes through. The door slams shut and echoes through the room.

"It was a person! They shouldn't be here," Dave says again.

"They could be dangerous! You shouldn't have chased them!" Jenna is saying.

"I only saw a shadow, not a person," you say.

"Same," Simon adds.

Jenna turns and says, "Josie? Do you know if that was ghost or flesh?"

You shiver at the phrase.

"That was a ghost," Josie replies, frowning. "A nasty one."

"That could slam a door?" Simon asks.

"Slam it, and lock it," Dave says from the other side of the room. He is pulling on the door that the shadow had gone through, but it won't budge.

"What do we do now?" you ask.

Jenna shrugs. "We keep investigating."

But Jenna doesn't have a chance to give out instructions before you are all distracted by a commotion coming from above in the stairwell.

"What is that?" Jenna yells. Everyone rushes up the stairs but stop on the landing when you find the stairs to the upper level blocked by what looks like random pieces of office equipment piled in a tangled heap.

"We're trapped!" Simon says. He joins Dave in trying to move the blockage, but it is so tangled and jammed in the stairwell that it is impossible.

"We're trapped," Dave says, resignedly.

Simon goes to the other side of the basement and tries the door, but as Dave had found, it won't open.

"What are we going to do?" Josie asks.

"Does anyone have their cell phone?" Jenna asks.

Everyone shakes their head.

"I'm regretting my rule of no cell phones during an investigation," Jenna says with a forced chuckle.

Hours tick slowly by as you all wander the basement. Eventually, Josie and Simon settle down against a wall. Not long after, Jenna and Dave join them and so you sit, also. You have all talked endlessly about the situation with no solutions; Dave and Simon have tried everything they could think of to force the door open and to move the furniture blocking the stairs with no success.

"Someone will come looking for us eventually," Jenna says with a yawn.

Eventually, you nod off and then slip into a deep sleep.

THE END

"Okay, Simon, don't hate me," you say. You take him by both arms, and you shake him as hard as you can while yelling in his face, "Simon! Wake! Up!"

He stumbles and blinks several times, shaking his head. "Whoa, what happened?" he asks just as your flashlight flickers back to life in your pocket.

"I was just about to ask you the same thing," you say. "You were standing there like a statue for like ten minutes!"

"It was the strangest thing – it was like I was dreaming," Simon says. "I was here, in this room, but it was a working factory, and there were people everywhere. So vivid and so strange!"

"Yes, I agree that the whole thing was very strange," you say.

"Okay, do you mind if we get out of this room now? I do *not* like it in here," says Simon.

"Yeah, sure, let's head to the break room," you reply and head toward the double doors on the far wall. Ahead of you is a short hallway with three doors on the left and two on the right. You stop walking suddenly when you see a light in the last room on the right.

"Hello?" you call out. "Who's there?"

A figure appears in the doorway, a flashlight in hand pointed at the two of you. "Oh, hey guys, I was wondering where you were!" Jenna says.

You and Simon look at each other, frowning. "Jenna? How did you get up here?"

She looks at you both in confusion. "What do you mean? And where were you guys?"

"We were in the big room," you say, pointing to the doors you just came through.

"I just walked through there, and you guys were not there," Jenna replies, firmly.

"You could not have walked through there without seeing or hearing us," you say.

"What is going on here?" Simon asks.

"I don't know. This place is insane as far as I can tell. So, how about the three of us investigate the break room for a bit since we're all here," Jenna says.

To investigate the break room, go to page 176

"I can tell this is important to you, Josie, so let's all go with you now and we can finish setup once I know more about whatever is going on," Jenna says.

"Good! Let's go," Josie says and starts down the stairs. Everyone follows.

But just as you all reach the first level, you hear a loud bang from down the hall and feel a rush of wind.

"Was that the front door?" Simon asks.

"Let's go check it out quickly," Jenna says.

You glance at Josie who doesn't object, so you head on down the hall with everyone to find that the front door has blown open.

"That's weird, right?" you say. "Do you guys think a person opened the door?"

"We would have seen and heard a person. A *living* person," Dave says. He approaches the door.

"Close it but do *not* step outside!" Josie says.

Dave and Jenna both frown at her. "Why?"

"Please just close the door and I'll explain," Josie says.

Dave forces the door to close. He then bolts it and shakes it to make sure it is secure. "Okay, if it opens again, we'll know something freaky is going on here."

"Alright, Josie, what the heck are you not telling us?" says Jenna.

Josie starts to walk back down the hall towards the stairs. "When we were on the second floor during my walk through, I encountered a man named Sam. Sam wants to help us." Josie then explains what he had said upstairs and answers Jenna's many questions about what he looks like and what time period he comes from.

As you all reach the dark, dank basement, Simon asks the same question you had asked earlier. "How do you know we can trust him?"

Josie looks at Simon in the light of the flashlights. "I just do, Simon. I *feel* that he is trustworthy and that he honestly wants to help us. I can't give you more of a reason than that."

"Well, I trust Josie, so I guess that means I trust Sam," Dave says.

"Me too," says Jenna.

Simon just shrugs.

Josie rolls her eyes. "Jenna, do you have the salt with you?"

"I do," Jenna says, swinging her backpack off her shoulder. She unzips it and pulls out a canister, holding it out towards Josie. "Here."

Josie takes the canister and pulls open the spout at the top. She starts to pour it out onto the floor, thick enough that you all can see the line. "I'm going to create a circle, and no one is to go inside of that circle under any circumstances. Okay?"

"You have to tell us why," Jenna says.

"I will, just give me a minute," she replies. She finishes making a large circle on the ground with the salt, then she squats down, places her palms flat on the ground just outside of the circle, and closes her eyes.

You all wait, watching her. All you can hear is the stressed breathing of the others and yourself as you wait impatiently for an explanation. Suddenly, the hairs on the back of your neck rise and a shiver runs up your spine, as though someone was standing too close behind you. You are about to turn around to look when Josie stands and says, "There are a lot of layers to this thing. I can go into more detail later, but what I am getting, both from the land below us and from Sam, was that there was some kind of battle here a long time ago, between settlers and natives, and there was a lot of bloodshed. A *lot*. This upset the land, and that upset created a kind of negative battery here, trapping a concentration of negativity in this area. Over the years, other bad things happened in this location as things 'plugged into' the battery. Murders, illness, conflicts… you know, the usual. As this building was being built, there were several deaths. A couple were accidents – falls and such – but there were also deadly fights among some of the workers. Once the building was completed, workers continued to experience bad things: the black widow upstairs, the little boy whose arm got ripped off—"

"Wait. What?" Jenna exclaimed.

But Josie continued. "Then the business closed down because of corruption and other illegal activity, and the building was abandoned. That's when the Satan worshipers came in."

"You can't be serious!" Simon scoffed.

Again, Josie went on. "They didn't know what they were doing. Well, mostly it was a bunch of stupid teenagers who thought they were cool, most of whom didn't think any of it was real. But there was one in the group who did, and who was dangerous. I won't go into details – I can't, really – but he used the people he was with, and he used the bad energy that was already here, and he created an amplifier. Whenever he wants to do more bad things, he comes back here, right to this spot within the circle. And if we go inside it, we may activate it and make things a lot worse here than they need to be."

Everyone is silent as you all absorb what Josie just said, and then Jenna finally speaks. "You're really serious," she says.

Josie shrugs. "I'm just passing along the information I'm getting. And, for the record, *nothing* about this place is a joke."

"Should we even be here, doing this?" Simon asks.

Josie shrugs once more. "I think we should try, but I think we need to be very careful. More careful than we've been at any other location. We could get in over our heads very quickly."

"That just makes me want to be here more," Jenna says.

"I know," Josie says, a hint of sadness in her voice.

"That means I'm not leaving Jenna's side for a second," says Dave.

"I would expect nothing else," Josie says.

"So, are we good to get back to the investigation?" Jenna asks.

Josie nods. "Just be aware of this spot on each level and avoid it if you can. It should be okay on the upper floors, but… well, just avoid it if you can. Better safe than sorry."

"Will do. Let's get a move on," Jenna says, the excitement oozing from her.

"I'll stay with Josie," Simon says, then looks at Josie. "If that's okay with you."

"Sure," Josie says flatly, but you think you see a hint of a smile in her eyes. Josie then looks at you and says, "Do you want to stay with me and Simon? Or go with Jenna and Dave?"

If you stay with Josie and Simon, go to page 4
If you go with Jenna and Dave, go to page 125

"What the—!" you yell, and another plate goes flying and smashes against the wall. Then another, and another. "Josie! Come on!" you shout and bolt for the door. You glance over your shoulder, but Josie isn't following you. You stop at the top of the stairs and turn back. You can hear things shattering still. "Josie! What are you doing? Get out of there!"

You take a step back, not realizing that you are so close to the stairwell, and you lose your footing. You tumble backwards down the stairs. Your head hits the edge of a step hard, and everything goes black.

THE END

You quickly decide that you do not want to be a third wheel to whatever is happening with Simon and Josie, and say, "I'll go with Jenna and Dave. Setup will happen quicker with three of us."

Josie says, "Okay, give Simon your camera and he can finish the walk-through with me."

You hand him the camera and look to Jenna for guidance.

Setup does indeed go quickly, but not because there are three of you; it is purely because of Jenna's boundless energy that you struggle to keep up with. Within fifteen minutes there are cameras set up in the basement, the large room on the second floor, the breakroom on the second floor, and in the tower room.

Once the camera is set in the tower and an audio recorder is running in a corner, Jenna says, "Alright, we may as well start our investigation here."

"Okay, what do you want me to do?"

"Well, let's all take a seat on the floor, and we can start with an EVP session," Jenna says.

You each take a spot on a wall where you have distance from each other but can still see one another. Then Jenna starts asking questions. "Is there anyone here who would like to talk to us?" "Who lived here in this room?" "Did you see things that frightened you here?"

On and on it goes. At one point, Dave asks a question. You try as well, but you feel a little silly and have trouble coming up with a question that hasn't already been asked.

Soon, you start to feel drowsy. You're so drowsy that you don't notice Dave has nodded off across the room and that the questions are coming slower and slower from Jenna because she, too, is starting to feel lethargic. None of you notice when each of you falls fast asleep.

You wake with daylight shining in the small, high windows of the room just as Jenna and Dave also stir to life.

"What the heck happened?" Jenna slurs with sleep. But sleepiness then turns to panic. Jenna and Dave grab the equipment and throw it in her bag as she calls on the walkie for Josie and Simon.

Simon's voice returns seconds later. "We must've fallen asleep," he says. "We're in the big room on the second floor."

"Please grab the camera in the break room and meet us in the equipment room immediately," Jenna says, already partway down the stairs. You hurry after her and Dave, almost falling as you trip over your own feet.

Everyone is breathless as you all congregate in the equipment room. "What the heck happened? We were doing an EVP session and next thing I know, it's morning!" Jenna exclaims.

Simon shakes his head. "Same here."

"I think we were not meant to be here," Josie says. "Sam says we should just go and leave this place to rot."

Jenna looks stricken at the suggestion.

"Babe, what else can we do? Our parents must be freaking out," Dave says to her.

Reluctantly, she says, "Fine. Ugh, I hate this place!" She stomps one foot in punctuation, and the whole building rumbles around them in seeming response.

"Okay, I'm getting out of here," Simon says and heads for the door. Josie is on his heels, and you follow too. Dave ushers Jenna out the door, their arms loaded with the equipment.

A week later over pizza, Jenna is scowling as she says, "I hope that place rots into the swamp sooner rather than later."

"There was nothing for evidence?" you ask.

"Not a thing. Every camera and every audio recorder is blank, like nothing even recorded. But I know we were recording," Jenna says.

"Well, we can't win them all," Simon says.

"Says the co-captain of the undefeated division A football team," Jenna scoffs.

"Hey, our soccer team has lost a few games," he replies.

Jenna rolls her eyes. "Okay, well, as much as I hate to admit it, that dang building has defeated us. But I'm not giving up completely. Are you guys ready for our next investigation?"

THE END

At the landing on the second floor, Jenna pauses. She unclips a walkie talkie from her waist and presses the button. "Dave?" she says into the walkie.

"Yeah, Babe," Dave replies.

"Where are you guys?"

"Break room – 2nd floor," he replies.

"Thanks, Babe," she says and replaces the walkie on her waist. "Okay, let's go to the tower and work our way down."

"Sounds like a plan," you reply, and she starts up the next flight of stairs, pausing on the landing of the third floor, to listen but you hear no sounds. You both continue up.

You reach the fourth level and stop when you see Jenna has stopped again. She is looking at a small notebook in the light of her camera screen. "Okay, the tower stairs are this way," she says and starts down the dark hallway before you.

"Is it me, or does it feel extra creepy up here?" you say. Your voice echoes around you in a way it hasn't in other parts of the building and goosebumps rise over your entire body. A shiver runs up your spine causing you to shake.

"It does feel different on this floor, doesn't it?" Jenna agrees. "It feels… thicker… and highly charged." As she walks along, she looks into each doorway with her camera briefly before continuing on. You notice that only one door is closed – the first door on the right.

"What does that mean?" you ask, unsure whether you want to know the answer or not.

"I'm hoping it means that we're in for more activity," Jenna replies. She stops walking and is standing before a dark doorway. Just beyond the threshold, in the light of your flashlight beam, you can see a steep and narrow wooden staircase that disappears around a bend. You shiver again.

"Are the stairs safe?" you ask. You know you sound like a wimp, but you are beyond caring.

"We'll find out, won't we," says Jenna.

You take a bracing breath in as she starts forward, and just when her foot touches the first step, you hear a loud moan come from somewhere above.

Jenna stops and turns to you. "Did you hear that?" she asks.

"Yes, I did," you respond, your eyes wide with fear, your heart pounding hard in your chest.

"What did it sound like to you?"

"It sounded like a person moaning," you reply.

"Male or female?"

"I think… male," you say.

Jenna is nodding. "I agree."

You wait for more. Jenna stands frozen, her foot still on the first step, as you both listen to the silence.

"Do you think it could have been the wind?" you ask.

"Shhh," Jenna says, her finger to her lips. She tilts her head so that her ear is angled up the stairs. "I hear whispering, multiple voices whispering."

Jenna then continues up the stairs, stepping as quietly as possible and pausing in between steps to listen.

You do the same, following her, stepping in the same manner, trying to listen over the sound of your heartbeat though you do not hear whispering.

"Hello? Is there someone up there?" Jenna calls when she is about halfway to the top. She then looks back at you. "I don't hear the whispering anymore. Do you?"

You shake your head but then you hear something. "Wait! I hear it but it sounds like it's down there," you say, pointing behind you.

Jenna frowns. "Typical," she scoffs, but continues up the stairs. She reaches the top and you hear her exclaim, "Whoa!"

You resume your slow, careful climb up the stairs, continually glancing behind you as though the source of the whispering voices may be following, and finally reach the top. When you look around, you join Jenna in gawking at the scene and also say, "Whoa!"

The tower room is a large, square space with high windows and a high vaulted ceiling with thick beams crisscrossing. Hanging from the center of where the beams cross is a rope that ends in a noose about five feet above your head. There is also an old, rusty metal twin bed with a bare and stained mattress in one corner, garbage strewn everywhere – fast food wrappers, beer cans and alcohol bottles, and dirty, discarded clothing – and graffiti covering every wall.

"Should we be concerned about this?" you ask Jenna as you shine your flashlight around the room, taking in the subject-matter of the graffiti. You see pentagrams, a cartoonish devil face, bubble numbers '666' in multiple places, and layers of other graphic and grotesque images of death and destruction. In one spot, someone had written "I summon the demon" but the name that came next is mostly covered by an alien face, a gray oval with large black eyes and a small slit for a mouth grinning menacingly at you.

Jenna shrugs. "To be honest, maybe. If people were coming in here doing devil worshiping stuff, the question is: did they know enough to be dangerous to themselves or to others?"

"Are you telling me that this stuff is legit?" Your heart jumps back into double-time.

"Yes and no. Can I confirm that the devil is real or that demons exist? Not for certain. But we have encountered some pretty dark stuff in our investigations, and Josie has helped some people who dabbled in this kind of thing and came out worse off for it."

"Wow," you say, unsure what to make of that. Then, movement above your head catches your eye. You look up and say, "Um… Jenna?"

"What?" she asks and when you don't say more, her eyes follow the light of your flashlight beam to the noose that is now swinging back and forth like a pendulum.

She aims her camera at it and says, "This is amazing!"

"What could be doing that?" you ask.

"No idea. But none of the windows are broken, so it can't be wind, and it's moving too much, too steadily to be from vibrations in the floor," she says. "Although I doubt our resident skeptic, Simon, would agree if he were here to witness this. Wait till I show him this video!"

You watch as the rope's trajectory widens its swing, and then it starts jumping, as though a giant's hand were plucking it like a guitar string. Jenna keeps making exclamations of excitement while you are frozen to the floor in awe and fear. And then, the rope starts to fall very quickly while continuing its swing. You can see that it is heading right for Jenna, and somehow it wraps around her. The camera falls from her hand as the rope coils around her body like a giant brown snake.

"Help me! Please!" Jenna yells.

If you run to get help, go to page 11
If you stay and try to get the rope off her, go to page 143

"Ugh, fine, let's try to get into the room," Josie says and looks to Simon. He hands you the camera and approaches the heavy wooden door. Simon turns the knob and pushes. At first, nothing happens. He then shoves at the door with his shoulder several times and finally, the door groans open with the sound of scraping wood and creaking hinges that echoes in the darkness around you.

A shiver runs up your body.

"Wow," Simon says as he looks around.

"Holy cow," you say as you step inside and take in the room. The walls are lined with bookshelves, many filled with what look like decaying leatherbound tomes, and an enormous desk sits in the middle of the room on top of a dusty though ornate rug. A single large leather chair is behind the desk facing away from you and you suddenly think of all those horror movies where some phantom is sitting in the chair that slowly spins around to reveal its gruesome visage to the unsuspecting victims. Your heartbeat starts to race as you watch Simon walk towards the chair. But when he reaches it, he puts a hand on the back and turns it toward you, and you see that once again your imagination is getting the better of you.

You move over to the bookshelves and shine your light over the dust-encrusted spines. Gold-foiled lettering still sparkles a little beneath the years of grime, but you cannot read what the titles are. You contemplate how to take one from the shelf but then Josie's strained voice comes from behind you. "Uh, guys? I think we need to get out of here," she says.

"Why? Does this room have anything to do with the guy we saw?" Simon asks.

She shakes her head. "No, but we need to get out of here right now!"

You jump at her urgency, but before any of you can move, the door slams shut with a loud bang. Simon runs to the door to open it, but it refuses to budge. He grabs for his walkie talkie, presses the button, but nothing happens.

"The walkie is dead," he says.

Just then, the camera in your hand beeps a low-battery warning and turns off, then your flashlight dims and goes out completely. Simon's flashlight goes next, and then Josie's. There is now only a small amount of light coming in through the two windows in the room, from the streetlights outside.

"I don't like this," says Josie.

"Everything with a battery is dead," Josie says. "He's drained all the power."

Her voice in the dark has an edge that makes you very uncomfortable.

"What does that mean?" Simon asks.

Josie takes a sharp breath in. "Give me a minute," she says, and you wonder if you can actually feel her frantically talking to a spirit guide or if it is just wishful thinking or your imagination.

"Okay," Josie says, finally breaking the silence. You can hear her moving away from you. "Let's all gather here, by the door but not against the door."

"I hate feeling so… blind. So… vulnerable," Simon says from within the darkness. There's a thud and an "Ow!" from him. "Be careful not to bump into the furniture."

You slowly make your way through the near-black room to Josie and Simon. You sit against the wall on one side of Josie with Simon on the other.

"My guides are here, and they've helped me put an energetic barrier around us," she says.

"Like the one around the guy in the tower?" you ask.

"Yes. The man that's here wants us vulnerable. He's dangerous," Josie replies in a hushed tone.

"Jenna and Dave will come looking for us eventually," Simon says.

But minutes pass and turn to an hour, then another hour. Every once in a while, Simon tries to open the door or tries to use the walkie or flashlight, but nothing happens.

"Josie, what is happening?" Simon asks. He has asked the question a few times already.

Josie's response is the same. "I don't know. This, whatever it is, is beyond me."

You doze off occasionally, as do Simon and Josie, and you start to wonder if you are all going to be stuck in that room for the rest of your lives when suddenly, a bright light fills the room. The sun has just risen over the trees and is flooding the room.

Then, you hear a loud click, and the door pops open with a squeal.

"Oh, my gosh! We're free!" you exclaim and hurry into the hall. Simon and Josie follow quickly behind you, and suddenly, Simon's walkie bursts to life with static and then Jenna's voice.

"Simon? Are you all okay?" Jenna says.

Simon responds. "Yes, we're fine. Where are you? We're still on the fourth floor."

"Second floor," Jenna replies. "Grab any equipment that's up there and meet us in the equipment room. I want to get out of here A-S-A-P."

"Got it," he says.

You all go back up to the tower and grab the camera and recorder that had been left up there, then head downstairs. You are all still unwilling to separate again.

"It does feel different in here, now that it's daylight," you say to them as you reach the bottom floor and head for the equipment room. Jenna and Dave are already in there packing up.

Jenna takes the cameras and recorders back and throws them in a bag. "Let's get out of here," she says.

No one says a word.

No one is sure what happened to you all, but no one wants to start the conversation. You all go home with no other conversation, only, "Bye, see you at school Monday."

But none of you ever talk about that night. Ever.

THE END

"Honestly, I'd just like to dive in and start investigating," you say, "before I chicken out again."

Jenna smiles. "You're eager! I like that. Simon?"

He shrugs. "I'm game. Let's head to the tower."

Jenna hands you both flashlights, then gives Simon a camera and you a walkie talkie. "Holler if you need anything. Good luck!" she says as you follow Simon out into the dark hallway. His face is partially lit with a pale green glow from the small LCD screen of the camera. You grip the flashlight tight in your hand, wanting to turn it on but unsure of what to do. Your heart is beating hard in your chest.

At the far end of the hallway, past many doorways that are darker than the dark hallway, you and Simon find yourselves standing at the bottom of a wide staircase. Nearby is a gaping hole of blackness, so you finally turn on the flashlight and shine it at the hole to find it is the staircase to the basement level. A loud, metallic-sounding thud echoes from below.

"Probably Dave and Josie," Simon says. "Ready to go up?"

You nod, finding your tongue is cemented to the roof of your mouth and your jaw is clenched tightly, rendering you unable to speak.

Simon climbs the staircase and pauses at the top landing of the second floor. He looks at you, then turns to keep climbing up to the third floor, then pauses again. You are breathing hard now.

"Do me a favor?" he says to you, the camera pointing directly at you.

Again, you nod.

"Unclench your jaw."

You are so surprised that you do as he says. Then he says, "Now take a big deep breath in, and then let it out slowly."

You do as he says.

"Good. Now, again," he says.

You do as he says and then ask, "How did you know?"

"I've done some training as a paramedic. I want to be a doctor. Reading the cues of a body in distress is something I'm good at."

"Oh," you reply.

"I know you're scared. And that's okay. It's normal. We're in a big, empty, spooky building in the dark. Who wouldn't be scared? But the reality is that the scariest things are in your mind. They are the anticipation of what *might* happen. Just remember that it is very possible that nothing will happen."

"But Jenna said—"

Simon holds up a hand to stop you. "I love my sister, but she can exaggerate things when it comes to the paranormal. And besides, you don't want to judge things based on what she says. You want to go into this objectively. You shouldn't be afraid because someone else says you should be. Does that make sense?"

"Yeah," you say, nodding, feeling your heart slow. "Thanks. I feel better."

Simon smiles. "Good. Okay, one more flight then on to the tower."

He continues up the stairs and you follow, feeling more confident. At the top of the stairs, you are surprised when there isn't a staircase up to the tower. Simon must see the confusion on your face, because he says, "This way!"

You follow him down another long, dark hallway. Again, there are open doorways, each one seemingly darker than the last. You expect something to jump out at you at moment and feel your heartbeat quicken again when you remember what Simon had said just a few moments ago, and you take a slow, deep breath.

"I can't believe how big this place is," you say, your voice echoing around you in a way that seems odd. "Does it feel different up here to you? Creepier?"

Simon shakes his head. "No. Not to me, but I don't really like to *feel* things in that way."

You frown, about to ask him what he means by that when you hear a whisper in your left ear say what sounds like a hissing, "Yessss!"

"What?" you say, jumping and spinning, pointing your flashlight all around you but you see no one. Nothing.

"What happened? Simon asks.

"I heard… I— I don't know. It was probably nothing. Let's keep going," you say.

"We're there," he says, standing in front of one of those gaping black holes that is a doorway.

You shine your flashlight beam over the threshold, and you can see a steep and narrow wooden staircase that disappears around a bend. You shiver.

"Are the stairs safe?" you ask.

"We should step carefully," he says, and starts up the stairs.

"That wasn't really an answer," you say quietly and start up, several steps behind him.

You reach the top of the stairs and enter the tower room. It is a large, square space with high windows and a high vaulted ceiling and thick beams crisscrossing. Hanging from the center of the beams is a rope that ends in a noose about five feet above your head. There is also an old, rusted-out metal twin bed with a bare and stained mattress in one corner, garbage strewn everywhere – fast food wrappers, beer cans and empty alcohol bottles, and dirty, discarded clothing. Graffiti covers every wall.

"I don't like this," Simon says as you shine your flashlight around the room, taking in the subject-matter of the graffiti. You see pentagrams, a cartoonish devil face, bubble numbers '666' in multiple places, and layers of other graphic and grotesque images of death and destruction. In one spot, someone has written "I summon the demon" but the name that came next is mostly covered by an alien face, a gray oval with large black eyes and a small slit for a mouth grinning slightly at you.

Then you notice the red light blinking from one of Jenna's cameras, watching you, and it makes you feel a little better knowing she has already been there.

"Simon?" you say, breaking the silence. "Should we go back downstairs?"

"Yes. No. We *should* do an EVP session, but…."

To go back downstairs, go to page 159
To do an EVP session, go to page 150

"Come on, quick!" Josie says and starts up. You are right behind her but then feel your foot catch on something. You stumble and have to catch yourself with your free hand. By the time you right yourself, Josie is out of your sight. You hurry, and when you reach the top, you see her going into the first room on the right. You follow her inside, but the door slams behind you and you jump.

"What the heck, Josie!" you say, but as you look around the room through the viewfinder, you realize that Josie isn't anywhere to be seen. You take in the room. The walls are lined with bookshelves, many filled with what look like decaying leatherbound tomes, and an enormous desk sits in the middle of the room on top of a dusty though ornate rug. A single large leather chair is behind the desk facing away from you and you suddenly think of all those horror movies where some phantom is sitting in the chair that slowly spins around to reveal its gruesome visage to the unsuspecting victims. Your heartbeat starts to race as you walk towards the chair, assuming Josie is playing some cruel joke by hiding behind it. But when you reach it, you find nothing but an empty chair. You look under the desk and see nothing but the dust-covered rug.

Frowning, you go back to the door and pull at it, but it won't open. You pound on it and shout, "Josie! Help!" but if Josie is on the other side, you cannot hear her.

Then, you remember the walkie talkie clipped to your waist. You set the camera down on the desk, unclip the walkie, and press the button. "Jenna, can you hear me? I need your help," you say.

"Go for Jenna. What's up?" her voice crackles back.

"Josie and I got separated. I'm stuck in a room on the fourth floor. The door won't open!" you say, trying unsuccessfully to keep the panic from your voice.

"On our way!" Jenna replies.

What feels like hours later – though you are sure it has actually been minutes – you hear a pounding on the door, then Jenna says over the walkie, "Stand back from the door."

"Roger that!" you reply. You are standing at the back of the room already, having been passing the time by looking through the books on the shelves. Moments later, after several more loud bangs, you hear the sound of splintering wood, the door flies open, and Jenna, Dave, Josie, and Simon come tumbling into the room.

"Are you okay?" Jenna asks you.

"Yes, I'm fine. Better now, though. Hey, Simon, when did you get here?"

"A few minutes before you radioed Jenna," he says. "She begged me to come help you guys. Didn't take long to understand why."

"How did you get in this room?" Jenna asks you. "It's been closed and locked all night!"

You explain what happened, thinking you were following Josie inside.

"That's interesting," Josie says, "because I thought you were right behind me the whole time. It was only when I got to the stairs for the tower that I turned around, and you weren't there."

"Well, look what I found in here while I was waiting for you guys," you say, and point your flashlight at a particular shelf of books.

They all move closer as Jenna reads the titles aloud. "Ancient Occult Practices. The Book of Real Magick Spells. Curses and Cures. Rituals of the Occult. Black Magick versus White Magick. Geez, no wonder this place is crazy!"

"The shelves are full of stuff like that," you say.

Just then, Dave leans back against the desk, and something goes sliding to the floor. He leans down to pick it up and says, "Guys, look at this!"

He has picked up what looks at first like an ordinary desk blotter, but on the reverse side it shows an intricately painted panel of numbers and letters.

"Holy crap, it's a Ouija board!" Jenna says. "Is there a planchette around?" She goes to the desk and starts to pull open the drawers until you hear her exclaim, "Yes!"

"I know what you're thinking, Jenna, and I don't think it's a good idea," Josie says, backing away from the desk.

"Oh, come on! You don't have to participate if you don't want to, but this is a chance for us Muggles to talk to the ghosts like you do!" Jenna replies. "Who else will be brave with me?"

If you want to use the Ouija board, go to page 171
If you don't want to participate, go to page 188

"Please! Help me!" Jenna yells again.

You shake yourself from your frozen state and tug at the rope, but it doesn't budge. You tug again and again. Then, you have an idea. "I'll go find Dave!"

"No! Don't leave me here!" she says, pleading. "Please!"

The fear in her voice causes you to stop at the top of the stairs and turn back. You go back to her and tug again and again at the rope with all your strength. Your hands hurt from the rope but finally it starts to loosen.

"Yes! It's coming off!" you exclaim and pull with renewed strength, trying to ignore the disturbing feeling of consciousness within the rope. You get Jenna's arms free, and she then helps unravel the rope from her lower body until she is completely free, and it is laying in a lifeless heap on the floor.

"Holy cow, that was insane!" Jenna says. She seems lighthearted but then she gives the rope a good kick, sending it flying across the room. She picks the camera up off the floor and points it at the rope, then scans around the room. "I'll have to come back up here with Josie later, see if she can tell me who did that to me!"

"How can a ghost do that?" you ask. "Or was it a demon?"

Jenna shrugs. "I doubt it was anything demonic. If it was, that was pretty pathetic," she says.

"Jenna, I don't think you should say things like that. You don't know who or what is listening," you say.

Jenna shrugs again.

"Okay, so what next?" you ask, trying to change the subject.

"I need to set up the camera and I think I'll leave another audio recorder up here, since we were hearing whispering and moaning." Jenna starts to pull equipment from the bag. She hands you the audio recorder. "Just hit record and find somewhere out of the way to put it."

You push the button and see the small screen light up and the numbers start moving, telling you that it is recording. "Tower room recorder," you say. You look around. There aren't many places to put it, but then you notice a shelf wedged into the far corner, almost invisible in the darkness of the room. You place the recorder there on the shelf, disturbing a thick layer of dust that tickles your nose. Suddenly, you get goosebumps again and feel the sensation of someone standing behind you.

"Um… Jenna?" you say without turning around.

"Yeah?" she replies, and you can tell she is still on the other side of the room.

"Can you see someone standing behind me?" you ask, trying to remain calm.

After a few beats of your heart, she says, "No, I can't see anything with my eyes or in the camera. What are you feeling?"

"Um… well, it feels like someone is standing right behind me, so close I can feel their breath on my neck," you reply. Then, you feel another sensation and say, "Ohhhh."

"What?" says Jenna. "What's happening?"

"This is so weird," you tell her. "It feels like someone is running their finger very gently down my neck and… oh… down my spine. It feels almost… sensual." What it does next makes you jump and shake your whole body, and you step quickly over to Jenna. "That was not okay! It just grabbed my butt," you tell her.

Her eyes light up. "Geez, this place just keeps getting weirder and weirder!"

"You are way too happy about this," you say.

"I will be more so if we actually catch any of this on camera or recorder," she replies. "Okay, let's head back downstairs."

To go downstairs with Jenna, go to page 154

You wake just as Dave pulls to a stop in your driveway.

"Good night! Thanks for giving me the craziest night of my life," you say.

Jenna chuckles. "I'll catch up with you in a day or two to teach you how to go through your audio. Bye!"

* * * * *

Two weeks later, everyone gathers at Jenna's house to go over the evidence that was collected. Dave arrives with several pizza boxes, and it smells like someone – probably Jenna – has made more chocolate chip cookies.

"Okay," Jenna begins, sitting with a laptop on the table in front of her while everyone else grabs a slice or two of pizza. "Thanks for coming. Even though we weren't there as long as I'd hoped, there was a lot of video and audio to go through. And I have to say that despite the insanity that we experienced, there wasn't much evidence caught."

"Seriously?" you exclaim.

"I was surprised, too," Jenna says. "But we did capture a couple of things. Of course, we got it on video when the dishes were flying through the air in the second-floor break room. *That* is probably our best evidence."

She turns the laptop around and hits a button. A video starts playing on screen. Everything is various shades of green – from almost a florescent shade to nearly black – but you can see plates, bowls, and cups go flying across the viewfinder and hear them shatter when they hit the wall. The camera view pans, and you can see clearly that there is no one there throwing the dishes.

"Wow," you say.

"Yeah," Jenna responds. "And you already know about the next piece of evidence," she looks at you. "After the first time we were in that room, as we were leaving, we heard a loud, clear scream."

"And you can hear it on our audio," you chime in. When you reviewed your recorder as Jenna taught you and heard it on your recorder through the earphones, it sent chills through your body and instantly took you back to the night of the investigation.

"On both of our recorders," Jenna says. "I want you guys to listen to it and tell me what you think." She hands Dave the headphones first. Everyone watches as he listens.

When he takes off the headphones, nodding, Jenna says, "Don't say anything until Simon and Josie have listened."

They each take turns listening, and then Dave says, "Yeah, that is a pretty clear scream."

"I agree," Simon says.

"Creepy," Josie says.

"Do you think it was Ellie?" Jenna asks Josie.

Josie shakes her head. "No, I think it was the little boy, Bobby."

"Hm. Okay. Yeah, I didn't get anything from Ellie, which I'm surprised by, considering how she threw dishes and harassed Dave," Jenna says.

"Do you think Ellie was the one throwing dishes and messing with Dave?" you ask Josie.

"Definitely. She was a nasty piece of work," Josie replies. "She was probably too out of energy after all that to create any sort of sound for an EVP."

"Was there any other evidence?" Simon asks.

"Yes, two possible EVPs, but… well, I want to get your opinions first before I say what I think it is," she says. "This first one is from Josie's recorder, from when she was clearing the swamp."

You each take turns listening to the clip through the headphones, which comes to you last. Jenna presses play. You hear Josie's voice say, "There is just so much sadness and confusion coming from these poor souls, it breaks my heart." There is one beat, and you hear what sounds like a whispery voice say, "Thank you," followed by Josie saying, "You're welcome!"

Your eyes widen in astonishment.

"What do you think?" Jenna asks you.

"It sounds like someone says, 'thank you' to Josie, and she responds back," you say.

"That's what I heard," says Dave.

"Me too," Simon replies.

Jenna and Josie are nodding. "We caught an EVP of a conversation between Josie and a spirit! Pretty cool, huh?"

"I'd say that's right up there with the dishes flying around," Dave says.

Jenna nods. "Okay, EVP number two. This one was caught during setup, but we were just walking through the hall on the first floor. And it was only caught on my recorder," she says, and the headphones go around one more time.

When they reach you, you listen, and frown. "Can you play it one more time?" She does and you listen, straining your ears.

"Well?"

Again, you speak first. "It's hard to hear, but it sounds like a whisper saying, 'shouldn't be here,' or something like that, but it's fast."

"I definitely heard 'shouldn't be here,'" Dave says.

"I heard a whisper but couldn't really tell what it said," says Simon.

"Same," Josie says.

"Can I listen again?" Simon asks.

Jenna passes him the headphones and presses play.

"One more time," he says. After listening to it again, he takes off the headphones and says, "Yeah, I hear whispering and it does kind of sound like 'shouldn't be here,' but it's really hard to tell."

"I agree," says Jenna. "I hear words, and it does sound like that's what it's saying, but it is hard to tell. Not a terrible EVP but not the best either. Josie, any idea who that was?"

She shrugs. "Probably Sam. He seemed the type that might try to warn people away."

"Interesting. Okay, well, it wasn't the investigation I expected, and it ended earlier than I would have liked, but our safety is first priority," Jenna says. Then, a big grin spreads across her face. "Alright, who's ready for our next investigation?"

"Count me in, Babe," Dave says.

"Me too!" you say.

"You know I'm in," Josie says.

Everyone looks at Simon. Finally, he shrugs. "Well… okay. Count me in, too."

THE END

"Well, I've never done an EVP session, so let's do that," you say.

"Okay," he says. He looks around, finds a spot on the floor, brushes dirt and dust away with his sleeve, and sits with his back to the wall. You do the same at a bit of a distance but not too far away.

"What do we do?" you ask.

"We can ask questions of potential ghosts and hope for an answer, but sometimes we get EVPs when we're just sitting around chatting," he says. "Since you've never done this, let's start with questions."

You wait.

Simon clears his throat and says, "My name is Simon, and my friend and I are here to talk to whoever is here with us. But we can't see you and we have a hard time hearing you, so we need you to talk really loud into these things on our arms." He points to his armband with the audio recorder. "Okay?" He pauses a few beats. "Do you want to talk to us?" He pauses a few beats again. You assume he is giving the ghost time to respond. You strain your ears for any voices or other sounds but hear nothing. "Can you tell us your name?"

After a few more moments of silence, he asks you, "Would you like to ask some questions?"

"Okay," you say, and then, "Can you tell us why you're here?" Pause. "What happened to you in this building?" Pause. Then you sigh and say, "This is hard. How do you know what to ask if you don't know who they are or what they're saying?"

"It is tough. We sometimes ask questions based on reports from the owners or on the history of the place," he says.

"Do you know any of the history?" you ask.

"Actually, Jenna did send me some info, but we don't know until Josie tells us what she's picked up on if this person is here or not."

You nod. "Understood."

"Okay, so, she found out that a man named Corey Sledge was found dead in this tower by someone when they were looking into doing renovations. Apparently, he was homeless and an addict, and they assume that he OD'd," Simon says. "With that being said, we'd like to know if Corey is here with us right now. Corey, if you can hear me, can you give us a sign? Talk into our recorders or make a noise for us."

The silence is weird and loud, like you are hearing the blood moving through your own body.

"Corey, can you hear me? I'd like to talk to you. I'd like to hear about your life," Simon says. Again, you both lapse into silence and listen.

"Okay, is there someone here who isn't Corey? Can you tell us your name?" says Simon.

More deafening silence.

After a few minutes, Simon says to the air, "If there is someone here who would like to talk to us, can you make a noise?"

Again, you listen. And you realize that the fear has disappeared and has been replaced with frustration bordering on boredom.

"This is really what this is like, huh?" you say to Simon.

"Yeah. A lot of sitting in the dark, waiting for something to happen. Let's try just talking to each other," he says.

"Sure," you reply. "What do you want to talk about?"

"Tell me about you. You're new to school, to our group…."

You shrug. "I don't know how much there is to tell. But I'm so glad to have met you all. It's made being 'the new kid' so much easier."

"Do you play sports? I can tell you weren't part of any ghost hunting club at your old school."

You laugh. "No, no ghost hunting clubs back home. No sports. I was on the school paper and chess club and hiking club."

"Ah! Good, hiking. That's how this all started for us. Did you know that?" Simon asks.

"No, I had no idea," you say.

"Yeah, so we were all at a summer adventure camp together – Jenna, Dave, Josie, and me although we didn't know Josie before that trip. But she and Jenna became friends on that trip. Anyway, there was a freak storm, and our raft flipped. We lost gear, Josie was injured, and we found a big, creepy house in the middle of the woods where we took shelter. That was when Josie started to see gho—"

The word is cut off by a bang from somewhere above you. You look at each other, quiet again, listening for more.

Simon breaks the silence by saying, "Is there someone here trying to get our attention?" He pauses. "Can you make that sound again?"

No other sounds come.

Several moments pass. "I don't know. It doesn't seem very active up here. Let's move on," Simon says and stands.

You stand, too. "Okay. What's next?"

"First, let's get out of this room," he says, and heads down the narrow stairs.

You follow him. You're at the top of the stairs when you feel something that feels almost like a finger brush across the back of your neck. You glance behind you but there's only darkness beyond the small beam of your flashlight, so you hurry down the stairs to catch up to Simon. You stumble a couple times, almost falling, and you scold yourself.

Simon is waiting for you in the fourth-floor corridor. "Alright, let's take a look in the rooms on this level."

To investigate the fourth floor, go to page 163

You follow Jenna back down the stairs. You almost lose your footing a couple times, so you step very carefully. You are still disturbed by the ghost-creep who was touching you and are happy to leave the tower.

You and Jenna are walking back down the fourth-floor corridor together when suddenly she stops. You stop and look at her. "What is it?" you ask with a frown.

"Were all these doors closed like this before? I don't remember them being closed," she says of the various doors lining the hall.

"No," you confirm. "I remember only the one up there being shut."

Jenna pulls the walkie-talkie from her belt and presses the button. "Dave?"

"Yeah, Babe," his voice crackles back.

"Have you guys been up to the fourth floor yet?" she asks.

"Nope, not yet," he replies. "Everything okay?"

"Yeah. Where are you?"

"Just finishing up the third floor," he says.

"Okay. Thanks." She clips the walkie-talkie back to her belt. "We'll have to come back up here later. I wish I had more cameras so I could set one up to watch the doors."

Jenna opens each door and peers in, then leaves it open. She reaches the last door on the front side and turns the knob, but nothing happens. "Hmm," she says, frowning. "We don't have time for this right now. We'll come back with Dave. He's strong. Hopefully he can get it open."

As you reach the third floor landing you pass Dave and Josie on their way up to the fourth floor. Jenna waves and blows Dave a kiss but continues downstairs. She stops again on the second-floor landing.

"Let's explore this floor," Jenna says to you.

You shrug and say, "Okay."

You follow Jenna through the double doors into a big room. In the darkness you can see some dark, distant shapes in the room. "What's that?" you ask.

"Looks like pieces of equipment. Must be whatever was too heavy to steal or too useless to sell," Jenna replies. "This must be one of the factory workspaces."

"That makes sense," you agree.

"Feels pretty empty in here," Jenna says.

"What do you mean by that?"

"Just that it doesn't *feel* haunted."

"Oh. Okay," you say, though you don't quite understand, and continue to follow. Double doors at the other end of the room lead out to a hallway lined with smaller rooms. You see labeled doors for men's and ladies' bathrooms.

Jenna stops in the doorway of a room at the end of the hall and says, "What the heck happened here?"

You hurry to where she is standing and look inside. As you pan the camera, you see a counter with upper and lower cabinets lining the back wall, several of the doors open or missing, a double sink breaking the counter half-way down, and at the far end in the corner stands an old, silent refrigerator. But the really strange thing is that it looks like there are broken pieces of glass everywhere. A shiver runs up your spine.

"I can't wait to hear the story behind this," Jenna says and steps into the room. The shards of glass crunch under her sneakers, then she looks at you and points to the floor. "This is why I told you not to wear open-toed shoes."

"What do you think happened here?" you ask Jenna.

"I don't know, but it was big. This room was not like this when I was in here earlier."

You both wander through the room, peering in the cabinets, looking at the walls and ceiling for you-don't-know-what. Occasionally, Jenna asks a question to the air, but the room is unnervingly quiet, and it is setting you on edge. You open your mouth to say something when a blood-curdling scream echoes through the halls.

"What the---!" Jenna turns back and pulls out her walkie-talkie. She presses the button and speaks into it. "Dave, was that Josie? What happened?"

The crackling voice of Dave comes back over the walkie. "Was what Josie? She's fine. What happened?"

Just then, another crackle comes over the walkie with a different voice. "Hey, where is everybody?"

"Yes! Reinforcements are here!" Jenna says, then into the walkie she says, "Dave and Josie, let's meet back in the equipment room and regroup. Simon's here to help."

"What about that scream?" you say. "Shouldn't we investigate that first?"

If you decide to regroup with the others, go to page 50
If you decide to investigate the scream, go to page 162

"Let's get the equipment from the basement first so we don't disturb Josie's work," Jenna says and quickly heads out of the room and down the hall.

You and Dave follow after her, trying to keep pace with her – a task much easier for Dave than you. And then, when you're halfway down the stairs, one foot catches the other and you start to tumble forward. You slam into Dave's back, catching him by surprise and sending him stumbling forward into Jenna, and all three of you end up in a pile at the bottom of the stairs.

"Ouch! Dave, you're on my leg!" Jenna exclaims.

"Sorry, Babe!" Dave stands up quickly, helps Jenna to her feet, and then does the same for you.

"Sorry about that. I don't know why I tripped," you say, as you each brush yourselves off.

"Maybe a ghost tripped you," Dave says and chuckles.

"That's not funny," Jenna says, her face ashen. "After what happened earlier…."

"Sorry. I'm sorry, you're right. Let's just get everything and get out of here," he says.

"Don't bother with how you break things down. Just do it fast. I can reorganize everything later," Jenna says.

You, Dave, and Jenna make quick work of it and move on to the second floor. Jenna is visibly nervous again, but you encounter Josie and Simon, and Josie gives a thumbs up and says, "All clear," pointing at the break room.

"Phew," Jenna says, then turns to you and Dave and says, "But regardless, I want both of you to stay here. You watch Dave and Dave, you watch me."

You both nod. Jenna dashes into the room, grabs the camera and recorder, and dashes back into the hallway as she stuffs the equipment in her bag.

"Last stop, the tower," she says.

You all make it to the tower and back to the equipment room without any further incidents. Josie and Simon get there soon after.

"Last stop, the 'Swamp of Lost Souls," she says.

"The what?" you ask.

"The swampy area out back. That's what I've been calling it in my head," she says. "I'm pretty sure it's been a dumping ground for bodies for a couple centuries at least."

You shiver at the thought. "That explains so much."

"I know, right?" Josie says.

"Alright, Josie, you take care of that, and we'll get the car loaded," Jenna says.

Once the bags are loaded, you get in the car with Jenna and Dave while Josie finishes her work with Simon standing by as her bodyguard. Jenna and Dave chat in the front seat. You want to join in, but you realize that you are exhausted. Before you know it, you are sound asleep in the back seat.

To gather for the investigation findings, go to page 146

"I don't like it up here. Let's go," Simon says.

"Okay," you say and head for the stairs.

"Why don't you give Jenna a call on the walkie and ask her where she wants us to go next," Simon says from behind you.

You do as he suggests, unclipping the walkie from your waist, but before you can push the button, your foot catches on something on the stairs. You stumble and drop the walkie as you try to right yourself. It clatters down the narrow stairs and breaks into pieces at the bottom. You shine your light on the stairs to see what caught your foot, but you see nothing.

You frown as Simon asks, "What happened?"

You shrug. "I guess I'm just clumsy," you say. You walk carefully the rest of the way down the stairs and start to pick up the pieces of the walkie. "I think I'll have to buy Jenna a new one."

"It happens to all of us," he says. "Let's head back to the first floor to see if she has any extras."

"Okay," you say, the pieces in your pocket now. You continue back down the long dark hallway, again expecting at any moment for some phantom to jump out at you from the dark doorways.

You descend from the fourth floor to the third floor, and hear a loud bang come from somewhere down the hallway. You look at Simon and ask, "Did you hear that?"

He nods and points his camera down the hallway. "Dave? Josie? Jenna?"

You listen, straining your ears for a response. Instead of a voice, however, you hear what sounds like fast-moving footsteps.

"What is that?" you ask Simon in a whisper.

"I… don't… know…," he replies softly, looking into the small screen of his camera. The sounds are rapidly getting closer and louder, like someone is running down the hall in your direction, and you expect to see someone come bursting from the hallway at any moment. Simon starts to move closer to the stair way, closer to where you stand, and then he says, "Go. Go! Go!"

He hurries down the stairs past you and you follow as quickly as you can, not knowing why. Simon continues down the stairs from the second floor, and you think you hear someone shouting behind you. You continue behind Simon, your heart pounding out of your chest, your throat hurting from breathing hard. And then suddenly you are tumbling down the stairs. You hear something snap in your torso and then in one of your legs as you fall head over heels again and again. Your head bounces off the stairs several times until you finally come to a stop on the floor. Consciousness is fading fast as you blink. You see someone looming over you. Simon, maybe? But you have one last thought before you completely black out: someone grabbed your foot and made you fall.

You open your eyes slowly to find yourself looking down at your own body, lying on the floor in a twisted and unnatural position. Simon is kneeling next to you, shouting though you can barely hear him. Then, the others are coming running towards you, flashlights bobbing in the dark, but they are looking at the you on the floor, not the you that is standing among them. You try to talk to them, but they seem not to hear you. Suddenly, there are blue and red lights flashing, overhead lights flip on, blinding you. You cover your eyes and squeeze them shut.

When you open your eyes again, it is dark, and your friends are gone.

"Hello? Jenna? Where is everyone?" you call out. You go to turn your flashlight on but it's no longer in your hand. You realize you probably dropped it when you fell. You crouch down and feel around on the floor, but there's nothing there that you can feel. In fact, you're not sure you can even feel the floor.

Panic rises within you as you realize that you are alone in the pitch-dark and something is very, very wrong.

Somewhere nearby in the dark you sense movement, and instantly your body vibrates with some unknown, unwelcome sensation. You hear your name whispered from somewhere within the shadows. You take a step towards the sound but then, you sense something else. You turn and see a light, just a pinprick, far down the hallway. Could it be your friends?

If you go towards the whispers, go to page 13
If you towards the light, go to page 228

"Let's investigate it on our way back to the equipment room," Jenna says.

"Okay," you reply.

"No idea where it came from though," Jenna says as she steps back into the hallway. You follow with the camera focused on her. "Hello?" Jenna calls. "Who screamed? Do you need help? Are you hurt? Angry?"

There is only silence as you walk on. She peeks into each room as you go by.

"Can you scream for us again?" Jenna asks, but you wish she didn't. It isn't a sound you want to hear again. Thankfully, nothing happens.

As you reach the stairs, you hear footsteps and voices coming from above and then Josie and Dave appear.

"Hey! We were just heading to the equipment room to meet up with you," Dave said.

"Were you guys in the break room when the stuff got broken?" Jenna asks them, pointing over her shoulder with her thumb down the dark hallway.

"Sure were," Dave says. "It was crazy!"

"Got any of it on camera?" she asks.

"Definitely," he says.

"Awesome! Okay, let's meet up with Simon and we can hear all about it and regroup," Jenna says.

To regroup, go to page 50

"Sounds like a plan," you say. You're feeling braver than before since nothing has happened to you that was scary. A bang that probably wasn't a ghost and a touch that probably was your imagination or your hair or your shirt, or anything other than a disembodied finger....

"Let's start down this way and work our way towards the stairs," Simon says.

You follow Simon to the far end of the hall and the two of you silently make your way through each of the rooms, moving slowly, deliberately. You are becoming accustomed to the darkness and the silence, and while you still wait for something to jump out of the darkness, you are no longer as anxious about it.

"What do you think these rooms were for?" you ask after emerging from yet another empty room.

"Probably offices," he says, then, "Look." He is pointing his light at the only door on this level that is closed.

Simon turns the knob and pushes. At first, nothing happens. He looks at you, then shoves at the door with his shoulder. The door groans open with the sound of scraping wood and creaking hinges that echoes in the darkness around you and you cannot help but shiver.

"Wow," Simon says as he looks around and you echo it a moment later.

"I guess you were right about there being offices up here," you say as you take in the room. The walls are lined with bookshelves, many filled with what look like decaying leatherbound tomes, and an enormous desk sits in the middle of the room on top of a dusty though ornate rug. A single large leather chair is behind the desk facing away from you and you suddenly think of all those horror movies where some phantom is sitting in the chair that slowly spins around to reveal its gruesome visage to the unsuspecting victims. Your heartbeat starts to race as you watch Simon walk towards the chair. But when he reaches it, he puts a hand on the back and turns it toward you, and you see that once again your imagination is getting the better of you.

You let out a huff of air.

"You okay?" he asks.

"Yeah," you nod. "Did you know this room was up here?"

He shakes his head. "No, no clue. I don't even know if Jenna knows about it. Let me give her a call." You hand him the walkie and pushes the button. "Simon to Jenna."

"What's up, Simon?" Jenna's voice crackles back.

"We left the tower and were looking around the fourth floor. Did you know one of the rooms up here is a fully furnished office?" Simon asks.

"What? Did I hear you correctly?" Jenna replies.

"There was one room with the door shut. We went inside, and it's filled with stuff. Nice stuff," he tells her.

"Stay there. I'm coming right up," she says, and the walkie goes silent.

"This is weird, right?" you ask him.

"Yes," he replies. "This is very weird."

You both move slowly about the room. Simon is looking through the desk drawers while you examine the bookshelves.

"The layer of dust on everything tells me no one has been in here in a *very* long time," you say.

"I think you're right about that," Simon says, though he is busy peering into one of the desk drawers.

Moments later you hear the sound of footsteps coming up the stairs. Simon pauses in his inspection and says, "probably Jenna," and you realize that he must be right.

A second later you hear Jenna say, "It's just me, guys!" From where you stand you can see out the office door toward the top of the stairs, and you see Jenna's flashlight bobbing as she comes up the last few steps. As she approaches, she says, "This is the one room in the whole building—"

BANG! The door slams shut in Jenna's face. She immediately jiggles the handle and pounds at the door. Simon rushes over and does the same from the inside, but the door isn't budging for anyone.

"Simon, what are we going to do? We can't be trapped in here!" you say, panic starting to rise within you. You look around, peering into the many shadows of the room where your flashlights can't reach, looking for the culprit, but you see nothing but darkness.

"We'll get out or we'll have Dave break down the door," he says, unclipping his walkie. Into it he says, "Jenna, get Dave up here and tell him to bring an axe if he can find one."

And just like that, the door pops open, stopping only when it hits the toe of Simon's sneaker.

"What the heck?" you ask, but you're grateful that the door is open, and you rush out into the hall as Jenna rushes inside. Simon plants himself in the doorway and will be hit again if the door decides to slam on its own once more.

"This room is amazing!" Jenna's voice floats out of the room into the hall. "Did you guys see all this stuff?"

"Yeah, Jenna, that's why we called you," Simon says with a bit of snark to his tone.

"Ledgers and record books! Wow!" Jenna says. Simon just shakes his head from his position as sentinel. Then you see Jenna appear in the doorway. "Okay, I want to put an audio recorder up here. Will one of you run down and get one? Or do you want to wait here while I go?"

If you volunteer to get the recorder, go to page 172
If you and Simon stay, go to page 192

Fear grips you, so you run, and Bobby follows. The two of you hide in the hidden nooks and crannies of the old factory until the voices of your former friends are gone. Afterlife soon slips into a never-ending oblivion, and you remain there in that run-down brick building with Sam and Bobby for eternity.

THE END

"I'm not sure I want to deal with Jenna and her questions just yet," Josie says.

"Okay, your decision," Simon says, "but at least tell the camera and recorders what you're picking up on so she can listen later."

"Right," Josie says. She takes a breath in, then pulls from her pocket a small tube of lip gloss and applies it to her lips.

A stalling tactic? Or nerves? you wonder.

Finally, she continues. "It's so weird. It's this huge pilar of energy, but… it can think for itself."

Simon frowns. "Like, it has its own consciousness?"

"Yup," she says. "And there's one more thing I should mention—"

But the sound of static and then Jenna's voice on the walkie interrupts her. "Simon? Simon, come in. Simon, where are you guys?"

"Hold that thought," he says to Josie, then into the walkie, "Basement." Simon says.

"We're on our way. You guys are never going to believe what just happened to us!" Jenna replies.

Simon walks towards you and asks, "How's your ankle?"

You flex it and roll it. "Better," you reply.

"Let's have you try to stand on it," he says and helps steady you as you rise from the stairs. There is a little twinge of pain when you put your weight on your foot, but it no longer feels unable to hold you. "That's good. But you should rest it a bit longer, just to be safe," he says.

"Okay," you say and return to your perch on the stairs.

Just then, you hear feet thundering down the stairs, echoing from above your head. Even though you're sure it is

Jenna and Dave, you feel the desire to stand and move away from the stairwell… just in case.

"Is it me or does it sound like a thousand people are coming down the stairs?" Josie asks.

"It's not you," Simon says.

You're relieved that they are thinking what you are thinking. "Maybe the other ghosts are coming with them," you say, and chuckle, but the look on Simon's face tells you that he is taking the possibility seriously. Suddenly your heart jumps into double-time with nerves, and you picture dozens of glowing white specters hurrying down the stairs behind an oblivious Jenna and Dave.

But when Jenna and Dave arrive in the basement, if there are any ghosts with them, you are unfortunately unable to see them.

Jenna rushes towards Josie and you stand and carefully follow, relieved that your ankle is feeling better by the minute. "You guys are never going to believe—" Jenna says, but she is cut off by a loud bang that echoes through the entire basement, and then the floor beneath your feet rumbles.

"What was *that?*" Dave asks when it stops.

"I found something unusual here, something I've never experienced," Josie says. She then quickly explains to Jenna and Dave what she had found and when she is done, they both stand with mouths agape at her.

"Wow, and I thought our thing was weird," Dave says, but then the floor rumbles and vibrates again. You have never experienced an earthquake before, but you guess this is what it feels like.

"Um, guys, I think we should get out of here," Josie says over the thundering rumble that echoes all around you. "Like, right now!"

If you run, go to page 35
If you stay, go to page 179

"I've never used a Ouija board before," you say, hesitating.

"All the more reason to try!" Jenna says. "Get over here!"

Her enthusiasm is contagious, so you step up to the desk. She has put a flashlight down so you can see the board.

"Dave? Simon?" Jenna says.

"Sure, Babe," Dave says, though he sounds a bit reluctant.

"I'll hang over here with Josie," says Simon, who goes to where Josie is hovering by the doorway.

Jenna shrugs and says, "Okay, place two fingers lightly on the planchette. Good. Okay. Who here would like to communicate with us using this board? Whose office is this?"

You wait for something to happen, feeling jittery and willing yourself to remain still. Jenna continues, "We want to know who you are, what you did here. You can tell us with this board. Did you use this Ouija board to help the business?"

Behind you, Josie lets out a cough that startles you, but Jenna continues asking questions. Then, through more coughs, Josie starts saying, "No, no, no, no, no, no, no! This is too much!"

"Josie?" Simon says, gripping her arm. "I don't think she's okay," he says, but Jenna is focused.

"The planchette just moved!" Jenna says.

"I didn't feel anything," Dave says.

"No, no, no, no, no, no, no!" Josie continues. She is now bent over, clutching at her head with one hand, gripping her throat with the other. "No! I have to get out of here!" She turns and runs out the door.

To follow Josie, go to page 226

"I'll go get the recorder," you volunteer. "Just tell me where it is."

"In the equipment room, in the big, black duffel bag there is a case with two more recorders. Bring them both, if you don't mind. Just in case," Jenna says. "And extra batteries! Triple-A. There's a whole package of them right on the table."

"Got it," you say.

"Here, take the walkie," Simon says, handing it to you.

"Thanks," you reply, and you turn to head down the stairs. Then you realize you'll be moving through the entire building on your own. You hesitate at the top of the staircase.

"You good?" Simon asks from behind you.

"Yup!" you reply without turning back, but your voice squeaks a little. To cover it up, you start down the stairs, pretending to be far braver than you feel. "Fake it till you make it," you tell yourself, but your voice sounds way too loud in the big open space of the stairwell.

You hurry down the stairs as quickly as you can while also being careful not to stumble. You feel as though eyes are on you the whole time and it is unnerving. You wonder where Josie and Dave are at that moment, but you do not see or hear any signs of them as you hurry to the first floor.

You make it to the bottom of the stairs, and you pause, eyeing the stairway down to the basement warily. The sensation that someone is there within the shadows, looking at you, is palpable. It is a feeling you really dislike, as though you are the unsuspecting prey to some vicious wild animal. You stand there, waiting for it to pounce on you. You wait. And wait. And nothing is happening. Then you realize that Simon and Jenna are waiting for you upstairs, so you head reluctantly down the hallway to the equipment room at the far end.

After a moment, you think you hear footsteps behind you. You stop and turn around, shining your light around the hallway, but you see no one. You continue on. After a few more steps, you hear it again – distinct heel-toe footsteps coming from behind you. But again, you see no one there.

"A-alright," you say to the air, to the unseen follower. "Wh-whoever is there, whoever is following me. Please stop." Your voice is shaky, and you are unsure. "Please? Just for now. When I'm with my friends, you can do whatever you want to do to scare us, but while I'm alone, please don't scare me."

You pause for a moment, hoping it worked, and continue on a little faster. To your surprise, you do not hear any more footsteps. You reach the equipment room and quickly find the two recorders and the package of batteries, and you turn to leave, but then you hesitate once more. It feels comfortable and safe in the equipment room. You don't know why. You haven't felt like that since the moment you started investigating. But you know Jenna's waiting for you, and you don't want to let your new friend down.

So, with a deep breath, you charge back out into the hall. You make your way steadily to the stairs, ignoring the feeling of eyes watching you from the many open doors as you pass, and you start back up.

You have just reached the landing between the second and third floors when your walkie crackles, causing you to jump, and you hear Jenna's voice over the radio say, "Hey, Noobie, did you get lost?"

You chuckle, your heart beating rapidly again. "Nope. Sorry, I'm on my way back. Be there soon."

As you clip the walkie back to your waist, you fumble with your flashlight. The beam points up and your eyes follow the light, and then you see the head and shoulders of a shadowed person peek over the railing from the fourth floor and then vanish from sight.

You frown, gripping your flashlight tight, and you take the walkie from your belt. Pressing the button, you say, "Hey, did you or Simon just look over the railing of the stairwell?"

Jenna's voice returns. "No, we've both been in the office the whole time."

"Josie and Dave aren't up there, too?" you ask.

Dave's voice comes over the walkie. "We're in the basement," he says.

Jenna returns, "Did you just see someone?"

"I think I did," you reply.

"Okay, get back up here ASAP!"

You run up the stairs, stumbling more than once, and when you reach the top, you see Jenna and Simon lit by their flashlights in the doorway to the office.

"Did you see anyone?" you and Jenna ask each other at the same time.

"No," she answers first. "Simon?"

"Not me," he shakes his head.

You launch quickly into the story of seeing someone peek over the railing. "But it was just a silhouette or shadow, I couldn't see any features," you say. "Did anything happen while I was gone?"

"Not a thing!" Jenna laments.

"But from what I could tell from skimming through one of the ledgers, something funky went on here. The numbers just don't add up," Simon says.

"Was it the guy whose office this is or was it someone else?" you ask.

Simon shrugs. "Probably the accountant or bookkeeper, and the head honcho here found out."

"Unless they were in cahoots with each other," you say.

"Cahoots? Honcho? I feel like I'm in an old western movie that dad likes," Jenna laughs. "Let's do an EVP session to see if we can find out."

"Okay," you say.

"Simon, you stay in the doorway. I'll stay in the room, and Noobie, you stay in the hall since you saw the shadow person out here. Sound like a plan?"

"Let's do it," says Simon.

You all spend the next half hour sitting on the dusty floors, alternating asking questions and listening to the silence, but nothing more seems to happen. All is quiet and still. You do not have the sensation of being watched anymore, and you're starting to get drowsy.

Finally, Jenna says, "Well, I think we'll call it for now. I'll leave a recorder up here, but let's head downstairs so we can regroup."

To regroup, go to page 215

"That's exactly what we intended to do," Simon says. "Let's go."

He follows you and Jenna into the break room. It's a large space with a row of cabinets on the far wall, many of which have their doors hanging open, and an old, dead refrigerator in the corner.

"Why is there glass all over the floor?" you ask as several pieces crunch under your sneakers.

As if in answer to your question, something goes flying across the room, missing your head by mere inches, and smashes against the wall. Glass shards rain down.

"As I said, this place is insane," Jenna says. "Want to try an EVP session?"

"Sure!" you reply eagerly.

Jenna nods and moves into the center of the room. She lifts her head and says, "Hello, my name is Jenna. I would like to talk to whoever is here, whoever is making the dishes fly across the room. Can you tell me your name?"

She pauses and you all listen to the silence.

"Why are you breaking things?" Jenna asks. "If it was to get our attention, you got it. Are you angry about something?"

Again, a pause.

"If you can hear me," Jenna continues, "can you make another sound? Maybe close a cabinet door? Or knock on the wall or cabinet?"

For the next ten minutes, you each take turns asking questions, wondering if your recorders are picking up anything. All you hear is silence.

"Well, nothing is happening," Jenna sighs. "Shall we move on to another part of the building?"

You and Simon agree and head back down the hallway with Jenna, peering into the rooms lining the hall as you go, finding nothing of interest. When you enter the large room, you brace yourself. Simon tells his sister what happened to him earlier. She is intrigued so you all stop and try another EVP session. You keep a close eye on Simon to see if he goes into another trance, but like the breakroom, it is quiet.

"Alright, let's see where Dave and Josie are," Jenna says. You then hear the crackle of the walkie talkie. "Dave, where are you guys?"

Dave's voice comes back. "Just got back up to the first floor. It was quiet downstairs."

"Okay, meet us in the big room on the second floor," she says.

"Roger that," Dave replies.

Moments later, Josie and Dave appear in the room behind a flashlight and camera.

"We had activity, and then it all went quiet," Jenna says.

"Same for us," Dave replies.

"Okay, well, let's go through the upper floors together one last time," Jenna says.

"Lead the way, Babe," says Dave.

For the next ninety minutes, the five of you wander through the upper floors of the building, then slowly make your way back down to the basement. The eerie feelings have subsided, the noises and shadows have vanished. All is quiet.

"Josie?" Jenna says as everyone files into the equipment room. Jenna turns on the overhead fluorescent light, a shock to your eyes after hours in darkness with only flashlights.

Josie shrugs. "They're still here, but it's like their energy went… I don't know, flat is the only way I can describe it."

"Can you clear it all?" Jenna asks.

"Easy peasy," Josie replies.

"Okay, let's pack up while she does her thing," Jenna says to the rest of you. You go with Dave to collect the cameras from the basement and then the second floor. After everything is packed, loaded, and cleared, Simon offers to drive you and Josie home. You both accept.

"I'd love to hear about how you clear a place like that sometime," you say to Josie from the backseat as Simon drives, letting out a big yawn.

"I'll go over it whenever we do the wrap-up from the investigation," she says.

"Okay, cool," you say.

You doze briefly until Simon pulls to a stop in your driveway. "Goodnight, guys! Thanks for an awesome night!" you say.

Your new friends give you a wave as you head into your house. Later, when you climb into bed, you feel happier than you have been in a long time. New friends and exciting new adventures have made life good.

THE END

"Wait!" Jenna says, "I think we should try to figure out what is doing this. Any ideas, Josie?"

"This energy thing – it's very unhappy that we're here and that I can see it and hear it," she says. The ground trembles again with thundering movement as if to confirm her words. You are anxious to leave and start to sidle towards the stairs, ready to run. "I think we should get out of here."

"But why is it unhappy?" Jenna asks. "We can't do anything to hurt it, right? Or can we?" Her eyes light up with intrigue just as another tremor shakes the foundation. "We can, can't we! How?" she asks over the rumbles, and then a chunk of ceiling falls and smashes at her feet. She jumps back.

"Babe, we need to go," Dave says, practically shouting.

"Josie? Can we stop this thing?" Jenna asks, shouting now over the cacophony. Another chunk of ceiling falls and smashes.

"I don't think so," Josie says. "I think we need to get out of here!"

Everyone hurries toward the stairs but then something that sounds like an explosion erupts. More chunks of ceiling rain down.

"Ow!" Jenna yells as something hits her.

You, being closest, reach the stairs first, but a giant piece of the wall above comes falling down. More and more of the structure above you collapses. You don't know what else to do so you slide underneath the stairs and hurl yourself into the furthest corner. "Guys! Under here!" you shout to your friends, but if they can hear you, you cannot tell, and before you know it, the entire building is collapsing. The stairs above you start to break, and a piece of wood falls onto your head and everything goes black.

* * * * *

You open your eyes slowly. Your head hurts and your mouth is very dry. The room around you is bright from sunlight coming in a large window. You realize you are laying in a bed, slightly propped up, and suddenly your mother is leaning over you.

"Thank goodness you're awake!" she says as you realize you are in the hospital.

Moments later several nurses are buzzing around you, saying things you cannot understand through the raging throb of a headache. You see one of them press something into the IV nearby, and very quickly your headache begins to ease, and your eyes become heavy with sleep.

When you next wake, you feel better. Both your parents are there now, and your father breaks the news to you that you are the only survivor of the building collapse because you hid under the stairs.

You become hysterical and moments later a nurse bustles into the room and puts another plunger of something into your IV that almost instantly calms you. As you drift off once again into a drug-induced sleep you say, "Life is never going to be the same."

THE END

"Let's start in the tower and work our way down," Jenna says. "I'll feel safer knowing Josie has already cleared a space before we go back in."

Dave looks at Jenna with raised eyebrows.

"What's that for?" she asks him.

"It's just that I've never seen you this… nervous in a place before," he says.

"Yeah, well, I've never had two of my investigators almost lured into a swamp before," she replies. "Let's go. I want to get out of here as soon as possible."

Jenna hurries out of the room with Dave on her heels and you struggle to keep up with them. You are huffing and puffing by the time you get to the fourth floor and your thighs are burning, but Jenna and Dave seem unfazed by the exertion and continue down the hall. They get a bit ahead of you, but you can see Jenna's flashlight beam and you know where they are going. Despite that, you feel a sense of unease again. You tell yourself it is just in your head, that being in the dark is uncomfortable on its own but add to it all you have experienced in a short amount of time and decide that anyone would be nervous. Still, you glance around and peer into the dark doorways and corners as you move as quickly as your body will allow.

You catch up to them at the doorway to the stairs just as Simon and Josie are descending.

"Easy-peasy," Josie says and gives a thumbs up.

"Great!" Jenna replies. "We'll be trailing behind you but won't get in your way."

You are grateful that it doesn't take long to get the cameras and recorders throughout the building. As you pass Josie and

Simon leaving the basement, she says, "We'll be out back. I have to take care of the 'Swamp of Lost Souls' before we go."

"Is that its real name?" you ask in shock.

"No, it's just what I've been calling it in my head all night. I think it was the dumping grounds for dead bodies for a couple hundred years or so," Josie says.

"Whoa," Dave says.

"Yeah, but down here is clear, so you're good to go," Josie replies.

"We'll meet you at the cars," Jenna says.

"It's okay, I can drive Josie home if you guys want to get going when you're done here," Simon says.

You exchange a knowing look with Dave that you are glad Jenna doesn't see.

"Are you good with that, Josie?" Jenna asks.

"Sure. I just want to get home and go to bed. I'm exhausted," she says.

"Okay, we'll catch up tomorrow. Thanks for all your help tonight. Both of you," Jenna says.

They leave and you help grab one of the two cameras. Back in the equipment room, you all take off the arm bands and audio recorders, gather everything together, and head out. Josie and Simon are gone by the time you three get to Dave's car. You climb into the back seat, and as he drives, they chat quietly. Soon, you doze off.

To gather for the investigation findings, go to page 146

"Let's all go up to the big room on the second floor," Jenna says.

Everyone stands. Dave shoves one last cookie in his mouth and gets a kiss from Jenna, and you all file out and head down the hall toward the stairs.

"It feels so different out here than it does in there," you say quietly.

Josie says over her shoulder, "That's because I put an energetic barrier around that room."

"You did?" you ask in surprise.

"Nothing can get in there right now," she continues, "except us and our guides."

"Why?" you ask.

"We've had ghosts mess with our equipment while we're not in there," Jenna says.

"Wow," you say. "I have so much to learn."

"Truthfully, so do we," Josie says.

You reach the stairs without incident, only with what now seems like the ever-present sensation of being watched, and everyone starts up.

When you enter the cavernous room, Jenna says, "Let's spread out and sit, somewhere you can see at least one other person, and let's do an EVP session."

Jenna and Dave head for the far side of the room. Simon and Josie each wander to separate sides of the room by the door, so you head for the middle of the room. There is a large, thick wooden post that you use as a back rest. Even though you can see the flashlights or camera lights of all four of your friends, you still feel nervous and vulnerable. You think you see shadows moving in your peripheral vision, but it is slight, and you are left wondering if your eyes are just playing tricks on you.

Jenna's voice cuts through the darkness. "Is there someone here who would like to talk with us?"

Pause.

"If there is someone here who would like to talk with us, can you make a sound? A bang or a knock?"

Pause.

"Is the little boy named Bobby here with us? I hear you like to play hide and seek. Is that true?"

Pause again.

"We would like to play with you, but we have a hard time seeing you. But I have a thing here with some colored lights on it. If you try to get close to it, it might light up different colors. See this, with the green light? I'll put it here for you…."

You can just barely see Jenna's shadowed form shuffle forward and place the meter on the floor. The green light seems very bright in the darkness.

"Bobby, can you try to play with the green light and get it to light up other colors?"

A couple heartbeats pass and then everyone, including you, gasps when you see all the lights on the meter light up.

"That's great! If that's you, Bobby, can you do it again?"

The lights light up one after another then drop.

"Good job! Bob—"

Jenna's voice is cut off by an enormous bang from somewhere overhead that seems to shake the whole building.

"What the heck was that?" Simon exclaims, jumping to his feet.

"They're all running," Josie says.

"What?!" Jenna says.

"The ghosts are fleeing!" Josie says.

"From what?" Jenna asks.

"Guys, I smell something…," Simon says, and hurries into the hall. You all do the same. He's looking up the stairwell, his light pointing up. You are imagining dozens of ghosts fleeing down the stairs around you. "Smoke!" he yells. "We have to get out of here! Downstairs, quickly but carefully. NOW!"

You do as he says, and he follows at everyone's heels. Now you know what real fear is.

"My equipment!" Jenna exclaims and tries to turn around.

"Jenna, this place is on fire, we have to go!"

His cell phone is against his ear, and he is telling someone – an operator at the other end of a 9-1-1 line, you guess – that there is a fire, and he is giving the address.

"There are five of us, and we are all leaving," he says into his phone. "The origin looks to be on the fourth floor, so we should be able to get out with no prob—"

Another bang from overhead cuts Simon off and you all take off at a run as you reach the first level. In the equipment room, each of you grab a bag and push through the door into the cold night air.

"Okay," Simon says. "Yes, we're out. Yes, we'll move away from the building."

From outside in the parking lot, you can see smoke billowing from the fourth-floor windows, and you are certain it is coming from the office you were in earlier.

Sirens can be heard in the distance, and you breathe a sigh of relief. Simon ends his call. You go to him and point to the window where the most smoke and some flames can be seen. "Looks like someone didn't want his secret to get out."

Simon's jaw drops. "I think you're right."

"All my cameras!" Jenna laments.

"The fire department is almost here," Simon says. "Most of your equipment should be fine. Except for the recorder in that office."

Jenna frowns.

The fire trucks arrive – two ladder trucks, an SUV, and an ambulance – and three police cars.

"Dave, you may want to call your mom and ask her to reach out to her friend," Simon says. "We're going to need to verify that we have permission to be here."

"Right," Dave says, and is immediately on his phone.

"What a crazy night," you say. "This is *not* what I expected."

Jenna laughs. "Noobie, when you're with us, you have to expect the unexpected.

* * * * *

Your parents aren't happy when they pick you up from the parking lot of the old mill building but are glad you are safe. You excitedly tell them all the strange things that happened during the night and somehow, by the end, they are no longer angry.

Jenna is allowed to get her equipment from the building a week later, everything except the charred recorder from the office that the fire department and police hoped would help in their investigation of the fire.

Several weeks later, you are all together eating pizza when Jenna tells you that they ruled the fire the result of faulty wiring likely disturbed during renovations.

"And what about the recorder? Or the fishy accounting books?" you ask.

"All burned to ash," Jenna says.

"So, we are the only ones who know Jeffrey's secret and we have no proof?" you ask.

"Unfortunately, yes," says Simon.

"Should we be afraid of him? Retaliation? That's a thing, isn't it?" you ask.

"Only in horror movies," Dave says.

"And besides, I crossed him over," Josie says.

"What? When?" you ask.

"When we were in the parking lot. I had to. There were so many of them, and they were all freaking out. He was reluctant, but my team was stronger than him."

"Wow," you say. "I have the coolest friends!"

THE END

"I've never used a Oujia board before, so I think I'll just watch for now," you say and go and stand by Josie, whose fear is palpable and more convincing than anything else that you should stay away from it.

Jenna just shrugs. "Okay, boys, let's do this."

Dave steps right up to the desk and places two fingers on the planchette just as Jenna has done. Simon hesitates, casting an apologetic glance at Josie, then joins Dave and Jenna.

"Is there anyone here who would like to communicate with us using this board? Perhaps the person whose office this is?" Jenna calls out to the air.

Beside you Josie stiffens and stifles what sounds like a cough. Jenna continues, "We want to know your story. You can tell us with this board. Did you use this to help the business?"

Josie coughs again, louder, but Jenna continues asking questions. Then, through more coughs, Josie starts saying, "No, no, no, no, no, no, no! This is too much!"

Simon turns. "Josie?"

"I don't think she's okay," you say, but Jenna is focused.

"The planchette just moved!" Jenna says.

"I didn't feel anything," Dave says.

"No, no, no, no, no, no, no!" Josie continues. She is now bent over, clutching at her head with one hand, gripping her throat with the other. "No! I have to get out of here!" She turns and runs out the door.

To follow Josie, go to page 226

The little blue flame light does another wiggle in the air, almost like a finger waggling to beckon you, and you cannot resist finding out what it is.

As you walk toward it, it starts to move. It is about five feet in front of you, hovering five feet above the swamp's surface. You follow it, keeping an eye on where the grassy ledge ends, and the swamp begins.

But then the flame-light moves further away. As it does so, it changes to a greenish color and then orange. It hovers near the silhouette of a dead tree.

"Who are you?" you call. "What do you want from me?"

As if in response, it wiggles again and then floats further along. You continue to follow even though it is getting further away. You see places in the swamp where there are areas of what look like solid ground. You step forward onto one, waiting to see if you were mistaken and get a soggy sneaker, but your foot remains dry. The light moves further away, and soon you are hopping from one mound of earth to another after it. It is moving swiftly, and you are going faster and faster to catch up.

What happens next happens so fast: your foot slips on some wet grass, the flame rushes at you, you lose your footing, and fall backwards with a splash into the cold, stinky water. You start to sink and then panic, flailing your arms to swim to the surface. You didn't expect the swamp to be so deep. Despite your efforts, your feet hit the bottom and sink into the soft, thick muck. You think, "I am about to die!"

And then, you feel a hand grab yours – a real, solid, fleshy hand, and the next thing you know, you are being pulled to the surface. You sputter, cough, and spit the disgusting swamp water from your mouth as you land on the hard grassy surface and then wipe mud from your face to see Simon and Jenna looking at you. Further back, you can see Dave and Josie.

"Are you okay? What happened?" Simon asks.

You nod, spitting some more muck from your mouth. "I'm okay. I don't really know. I saw this light and…." You stop talking, suddenly realizing how foolish it sounds.

"A ghost light!" Jenna exclaims.

"Let's get you back to the parking lot. I have a blanket in my car," Simon says. He escorts you carefully back through the maze of raised mounds of earth in the swamp to the solid shore. You are shivering from your wet clothes. "I think you should call your parents and call it a night," he says.

"Yeah, I think you're right," you agree as he wraps you in a blanket. Thankfully, your cell was in your bag inside. Jenna retrieves it for you, and you call your parents. They agree to come get you. "How did you know where I was?" you ask when you hang up.

"We thought you were taking too long using the bathroom, so we came looking for you," Simon says. "Jenna saw your flashlight heading for the swamp."

"Did you guys see the dancing flame?" you ask.

They all look at each other and Jenna responds, "No, we didn't see it."

"But there are a lot of dead people out there," Josie says. "I think people used to use this as a dumping ground for their bad deeds."

You shiver again, but not from your wet clothes.

Your parents arrive and you thank Simon for saving your life. "Please call me tomorrow and let me know how the rest of the investigation goes," you say to Jenna.

"Will do! Go get dry!" she replies, and they wave as you drive off with your parents.

THE END

"I'd like to stay here, if that's okay," you say.

Jenna shrugs. "No problem. I'll run and grab a recorder and be right back," she says and hurries off. You can hear her footsteps as she descends the stairs back to the first floor.

"What should we do while we wait for her?" you ask.

"Let's keep looking through stuff," Simon says, and he returns to the desk.

"Aren't you worried that the door will slam shut again?" you ask.

"Not really. If it does, I'm sure it will open again, just like it did before," he said. You can't help but admire how calm and cool he remains.

Everything falls quiet except for the sounds of Simon as he continues to look through the desk. You don't want to just stand around, so you go back to the bookshelves and open the book you had been looking at earlier. Its pages were lined with columns of hand-written information in ink that was faded in places, but you can make out names, dates, and numbers that appear to be dollar amounts.

"I think this is a record of employees and wages," you tell Simon.

He walks to where you are and peers at the pages you hold open for him. "It's crazy to think that people used to have to track all that by hand," he says, and he starts pulling down other similar books and browses through the pages. "This one looks like production records and sales," he says, but he is frowning deeply.

You look through another book but are unable to decipher what it was for. "This one makes no sense. It's just a lot of abbreviations and numbers, but I can't make heads or tails of it. Can you?" you ask and hand the book over to him.

He takes it and looks through a few pages, then takes it to the desk with the book he was already looking at. His frown deepens as he looks from one book to another, laying open on the desk before him, the light from his flashlight going back and forth. You just watch, like a glow-in-the-dark tennis match.

A few more minutes pass where the only sounds are the flipping of pages and a couple grunts of confusion or concern from Simon, then finally he says, "Something is not adding up here. I think something fishy may have been going on."

You are just about to ask for more information when you hear a loud, "Ha ha!"

"Did you hear that?" Simon asks, looking at you.

"Yes!"

"A laugh?" he asks.

"Yes, I heard a laugh. Sounded like a man to me," you say.

"That's what I heard, too," he says.

Just then, you see movement out in the hallway, and then what looks like a person peek into the room and then vanish again. "Who was that?" you ask and hurry to the door. You look into the hall, shining your light down the hallway, but no one is there. Jenna and her flashlight come bounding up the stairs.

"What's going on?" she asks.

Simon responds, "We were going through the books in there, and then we heard a laugh."

"Then I saw what looked like someone peeking into the room," you add.

"What?? I always miss the best things!" Jenna laments.

"Sorry, Jenna," you say.

Simon says, "Sorry you missed it. But hopefully we caught the laugh on audio."

"It was loud enough," you say.

"And when it happened, I was just saying that I may have found evidence in the ledgers that something fishy was going on in this place with the financials," Simon adds.

"Well, let's do an EVP session," Jenna says, frustration obvious in her tone. "Maybe something else will happen."

"Okay, I think I'll hang out in the doorway in case the door decides to slam again," Simon says.

"And one of us should sit in the hallway while the other one stays in here," Jenna says.

"I'll take the hallway," you offer.

"Let's do it," says Simon.

You all spend the next half hour sitting on the dusty floors, alternating asking questions and listening to the silence, but nothing more seems to happen. All is quiet and still. You do not have the sensation of being watched anymore, and you're starting to get drowsy.

Finally, Jenna says, "Well, I think we'll call it for now. I'll leave a recorder up here, but let's head downstairs and regroup."

To regroup, go to page 215

"I have a bad feeling about that room," Josie replies, eyeing the door nervously like it is a wild animal being held by a weak chain. "Which means we *need* to investigate it. But let's come back. I don't want to open that can of worms yet until I figure out this other thing."

"Sounds fair," you say with a shrug and continue following them down to the third level. Josie goes down the hall to the second door on the left. Simon follows her inside, while you linger in the doorway.

You both watch Josie as she walks through the room with a frown on her face. Every now and then she says, "Hmm," and continues on.

When she rushes from the room again, you look at Simon who just shrugs and follows, so you do the same. Josie hurries down to the second floor and into the big room. She moves to a spot and looks up, looking or feeling for something. She nods, and again, hurries from the room. She continues down the stairs to the first floor and heads for the second door on the left.

"Josie, talk to us," Simon finally says as she stands in the middle of the room looking up and down.

"I will," she says. "But… I need to check one more place." She once again hurries from the room for the stairs and heads down into the basement. You hesitate at the top of the stairs but decide that you've come too far to stop now, and you rush to catch up. Then, halfway down, you feel your foot catch on something hard and suddenly you are flying forward. A cry fails to escape your open mouth as you see the cement floor growing increasingly close and you land with a jarring thud and tumble a couple times before coming to a stop at Simon's feet.

"Are you okay?" he asks, immediately putting the camera down and kneeling at your side.

You roll over and he helps you sit up. "I think I'm okay," you say. "I'll be bruised tomorrow, though."

"Okay, let's get you to your feet," he says and takes both your hands, but when you put weight on both feet, your right ankle gives out and you nearly collapse as you yelp with pain. "Oh no, you might have a sprain. Let's have you sit on the stairs," he says, helping you hop to the stairwell. "Stay here while I help Josie," he says, and heads off into the dark basement.

You can see their flashlights and the light of the camera, but they are far away, and you once again find yourself feeling very vulnerable.

But curiosity gets the better of you as you replay your fall in your mind. Your foot hit something that felt very solid, so you turn around and shine your light up the stairs at the point where you think you tripped, but you see nothing.

"Hm," you say to yourself and turn back toward where Josie and Simon are standing.

"Now can you tell us what's going on?" Simon says to Josie. His voice echoes in the large, empty space.

"I'll try, but it's weird," she starts. "It's like there's a column of energy running up through this entire place in this spot, and it's pretty big. Like, maybe twenty feet in diameter. And it's different than the energy in the rest of this place but…."

"But what?" Simon urges.

Josie looks at Simon and puts her hands on her hips. "Simon, this is going to sound completely insane."

"Josie, I've been around you and Jenna enough—"

"That's not what I mean, Simon," Josie cuts him off. "I mean, even for me. Even for Jenna. This is unlike anything I've encountered before."

"Should we get Jenna and Dave down here before you go any further?" he asks.

If you think he should call Jenna and Dave, go to page 28
If you think he should not call them, go to page 168

"Well," you begin, "I don't think it's my place to make the decision, but in my opinion, I'm not sure I like the idea of any of us going anywhere on our own after what nearly happened to me outside."

Dave frowns in thought and says, "You have a point. I'll just hang out here in the hallway then, okay?"

Jenna says, "I think that's a good compromise."

"Okay, I'll be in the hall," he says, kisses Jenna on the cheek, and leaves the room.

You slowly make your way over to Jenna and say quietly, "Is the ghost trapped in this room? Can't she harass him out there, too?"

"Yes, theoretically. If the ghost believes she can go into the hall, then she can go into the hall," she replies.

"Does Dave know this?" you ask.

She nods. "He's done this enough, he should know." Then she shrugs. "Alright, let's continue with the EVP session." She turns toward the center of the room and says, "Hey, Ellie. We'd like to talk to you, if that's okay. We would like to know your story."

She pauses for a few beats.

"We've heard you murdered some men, but I figure you probably see things differently. Can you tell us what happened? What is *your* side of the story?" Jenna pauses again.

You find her approach interesting. Smart. Trying to get on her good side.

Jenna continues after a short silence. "If you did hurt someone, I'm guessing they did something to deserve it. What did they do to you?" Pause. "How did those men hurt you, Ellie? We want to hear your side of it. That's only fair, right?"

She pauses again.

You start to move slowly through the room. "It doesn't feel like it did in here when Dave was in here," you say quietly.

"You're right," she says. She turns toward the doorway. "Hey, Babe? I think we're done in here."

She is answered by only silence. "Babe?" she repeats and heads to the door, her flashlight held before her. She gets to the jamb and turns to you. "He's gone."

Jenna takes off down the hall, shouting for him. "Dave! Where are you? This isn't funny!"

You follow her as she flies down the stairs to the first floor, almost losing your footing in the dark several times.

When she reaches the bottom, she says, "I see him! Dave! What are you doing? Answer me!"

She dashes down the hall at full sprint, and you are following as fast as you can. By the time you catch up with her, she has followed Dave outside, and you have to stop and bend over, huffing and puffing, trying to catch your breath and to stop the stitch in your side.

"Dave! What are you doing?" Jenna yells, grabbing at him, but he is standing stationary like a statue, looking out at the swamp. "Dave!"

She is shaking him by the arm, but he isn't responding. Then, you see her pull her arm back, and you hear a crack as her palm meets his cheek. It echoes through the night. Dave comes suddenly back to life.

"Ow, Babe, why'd you hit me?" Dave asks, rubbing his cheek. He looks around. "Why are we outside?"

"I'll tell you as we head back in, okay?" she says, taking him by the arm and leading him back inside.

As you all have some water and another cookie, you learn that the last thing Dave remembers before the slap is that he had the thought that he needed to use the bathroom, thought about running outside to do so, then he heard something behind him, so he turned to look, but remembers nothing else.

Jenna is shaking her head and her voice is thick. "We could have lost you. What if you had walked into that swamp? I can't even think about it."

"I'm fine, Jenna," he says, and he pulls her into an embrace, but the look on his face tells you that he is just as shaken as she is at what happened.

She sniffles in his arms and pulls back. "I'm calling it a night. This place is too… well, too much for the five of us." She unclips her walkie and presses the button. "Josie, Simon, I'm ending the investigation."

Josie's voice comes back. "Is everything okay?"

"Yes, but it almost wasn't. What do you need from me to clear this damned place?"

"Simon can stay with me as I do it, Jenna," Josie replies. "You guys can break down the equipment while I clear. It shouldn't take too long."

"Sounds like a plan," Jenna says with a sigh of relief, and returns the walkie to her waist.

If you go to the basement first, go to page 157
If you go to the tower first, go to page 181

"Let's split up again," Jenna says. "Noobie, you go with Josie and Simon. Maybe you guys can head down to the basement and learn more about the nasty guy. And Dave and I will go up to visit the 'Black Widow'. Okay?"

"Let's go," says Simon.

You follow Simon and Josie out into the hallway and shiver. Once again you feel like there are eyes on you. "Is there a method to how she splits up the teams?" you ask to break the creepy silence.

Josie answers, "Not really. We investigate as one big group or split up. We have all investigated with each other at some point. It all depends on the place."

You reach the gaping black hole that is the stairwell to the basement and shiver again. Josie is standing next to you and says, "Yeah, I don't like it down there, either."

All three of you are tense as you descend the stairs. Though everyone has their flashlights lit, the combined beams don't go far into the gloom. You wander, though not going too far from Josie or Simon, looking around at the space. It is large and mostly empty except for large posts set at regular intervals, likely at least partially responsible for keeping the building standing. What little ambient light that made its way into the upper floor windows from nearby light posts outside was not able to find a single hole or window into the basement. Your flashlight beam reflects off the lens of a camera Jenna has set up and at first it makes you jump, thinking it was the reflective eye of a Cyclops. The air is heavy with that smell most basements have of mustiness combined with years and years of dust which makes you sneeze.

"Bless you," Simon and Josie both say.

"Thank you," you say, sniffling. "So, Josie, do… do you see him? Am I allowed to ask that?"

"At this point, yes, you can ask that and no, I don't see him, but I know he's here somewhere," she replies.

"You said he was dumped in the swamp out back but hangs out here?" Simon asks.

"Yes," she replies. "And I don't think he was the only one."

"The only one what?" you ask.

"Killed and dumped in the swamp," she says. Again, you shiver.

"There's a door over here," Simon says. He is at the back side of the expansive room. "A bulkhead."

You hear the clanging and then a screeching protest of metal as he opens the door. A rush of fresh air reaches you.

"Simon, where are you going?" Josie asks from behind you as you both follow him up and out of the basement, and you are happy to be out of there.

You look around. There is some ambient light from the street lights on the other side of the building, but it is still dark, however you can see that there is about six feet of grass before it drops off into the swamp.

"Swamps always give me the creeps," you say.

"You're very energetically perceptive," Josie says. "Swamps are stagnant water, which means stagnant energy. A lot of bad energetic stuff gets stuck in swampy areas."

"Really?"

"Especially if there's been multiple bodies dumped in it," Simon says. "I can feel it, too, and it is nasty."

"You feel stuff, too?" You ask him.

"Simon's an Empath, so yeah, he just doesn't like to admit it," Josie says. You can tell she is teasing him.

"It's not that I don't want to admit it, it's just that I'd rather find the science behind it all," Simon says, unfazed by her teasing.

"That's fair," you reply.

Suddenly, from behind you, you hear loud bang that seems to shake the entire building.

"What the heck was *that?*" Josie exclaims.

Simon is quickly on his walkie. "Jenna, Dave, are you guys okay?"

"Yeah," Jenna's voice comes back. "It sounded like it came from above us."

"I don't like that sound," Simon says back into the walkie. You silently agree.

"Hold on, Simon, Dave thinks he—" The walkie cuts out.

"Simon, there's smoke! Coming from somewhere above us!" Jenna's voice comes in a panic. "Get out!"

"We are already out, we're out back. You guys need to get out here right now!"

Another loud bang shakes the building as you, Josie, and Simon hurry around to the front. Jenna and Dave come bursting from the door to the equipment room just as you reach the side, laden with Jenna's equipment bags. You and Josie each grab a bag and put them in the car while Simon speaks into his phone.

"Yes, fire. Fourth level," he is saying. Then pauses. "No, we're all out of the building,"

"I still have so much equipment in there," Jenna laments.

"I'm sure it will be fine, Babe," Dave says. "I'm just glad we're all safe."

"It looks like the fire is in the office," you say, pointing to the one window on the fourth level with visible flames.

"I guess someone didn't want his secret to be discovered," Simon says to you. Then into the phone he says, "Yes, I can hear the sirens. They're close."

The fire trucks arrive – two ladder trucks, an SUV, and an ambulance – and three police cars.

Simon walks over to the SUV immediately and approaches the man that gets out of the driver's side. "Chief Mason, I'm glad you're here."

"Simon knows the fire chief?" you ask.

"Simon knows a lot of the first responders," Jenna says. "He wants to be an ER doctor, so he does a lot of volunteer work, CPR and first aid classes with them."

"Oh," you say as Simon and the chief approach.

"Dave, can you get in touch with your mom's friend?" Simon asks. "We're going to need her to verify we have permission to be here."

"And you kids will also want to call your parents," Chief Mason says.

Your parents arrive and at first are mad and worried, then they are fascinated as you all tell the stories of the night and of finding suspicious records in the office.

The Chief approaches where you are all gathered – friends and parents. "The fire hadn't spread beyond the office, and we were able to put it out quickly, but it looks like those records you spoke of are ash," he says.

Jenna and Simon are both visibly disappointed. "What about my equipment?" Jenna asks. "Can I go get it?"

"We need to complete our investigation and ensure the building is safe, and then you can get your stuff. It'll be a few days," he says. "You all go home now and get some sleep."

As you are saying goodbye to your new friends you say, "Thanks, guys! This was the best night of my life!"

* * * * *

A few weeks later, Jenna invites everyone to her house for pizza and an evidence reveal. She had retrieved all her equipment except the recorder in the office which had been destroyed.

"First, Josie…," Jenna says.

Josie takes a deep breath in and says, "I was able to cross everyone over."

"What? When?" you ask.

"I did some that night in the parking lot. But there were so many of them, and they were freaking out, but I was so tired. So, I did the ones that were most frightened, then did the rest when I went with Jenna to get her equipment. Some did go on their own, too. But Jeffrey, Bobby, and Sam were all rather stubborn. Thankfully, my team is awesome, and we eventually got them all to go."

"I have so many questions…," you say.

"I have no doubt, but we can go over that later, okay?" Jenna says.

Josie rolls her eyes at Jenna and winks at you as you say, "Yeah, of course."

"Okay, so," Jenna goes on. "We caught several EVPs and anomalous sounds on different recorders. Movement in the big room, like machinery, though the room is practically empty, footsteps in the basement. But there are some voices, too. Here's the first one."

She presses the play icon on her computer screen that displays a long line of green spikes on a black background, showing where sound is in the track. You all lean forward and listen. You hear what sounds like two male voices talking.

"I can't make out what they're saying," Dave says.

"Yeah, it's too faint," says Jenna. "This came from the recorder I left in the tower. None of us were anywhere near that recorder at the time. Okay, here's the next one."

Again, you all lean forward just a little more. The first two words are hard to hear but you think it says, "Get out!" Followed by… "Did that just say the 'B' word?" you ask, not willing to repeat it.

"Yes," Jenna says, her eyes lit with excitement. "And did it sound male or female to you?"

"Female," you say, and everyone else agrees.

"That was captured on my arm band recorder in the second-floor break room," she says. "I think it was the 'Black Widow' woman!"

"Makes sense," Simon says.

"Okay, and this next one is the best one and comes from our newest team member," Jenna continues.

You already know what it says; you were shocked when you heard it while reviewing your evidence, after hours of hearing nothing but your own voice and the voices of your friends. Jenna presses play.

There is a moment of static, and then a sweet, soft voice says, "Don't go… stay with me and play!"

All the hairs on your body are standing up and a shiver runs up your spine and shakes your body just like it did every other time you listened to it.

Josie is nodding. "Bobby," she says. "Poor kid. I'm glad I was able to cross him over."

"That is the creepiest thing ever," Dave says.

"This was one heck of an investigation," Simon says.

"Are you guys ready for the next one? I just got a call today," Jenna says.

"Yes!" you reply enthusiastically.

THE END

You look at Dave like a deer in the headlights. "I… I don't think this is a decision I should make," you say.

Dave shrugs, looks at Jenna, and says, "I don't want to leave you guys but… I'm just not comfortable here."

"Babe, it's fine. We will be fine," Jenna says.

"I'll just take a breather, have some water back at the room. I'll be gone ten minutes at most. Okay?" Dave says.

"Yeah, ten minutes. Sounds good," Jenna replies, and Dave disappears down the hall into the darkness.

Jenna turns and starts walking through the room again and you say, "Is he okay?"

"I'm sure he's fine. Everyone needs to take a break now and then," she says, but you suspect she is worrying about him.

"Want to keep doing the EVP session?" you ask.

"Yes, let's do that. I'll start." She pauses and then says, "Hey, Ellie. So, you like my boyfriend, huh?"

Pause.

"Well, guess what. He would never look at someone as ugly as you."

Pause.

"It's not just your looks that are ugly. You could be a supermodel – not that you know what that means – but you're ugly inside, too, aren't you?"

Pause.

"Did killing men really make you feel good about yourself?"

Pause.

"How long would that 'high' last? I'm guessing not long, which is why you had to keep killing."

Pause.

"Do you realize what a sick human being you are?"

Pause again.

You are growing increasingly uncomfortable with Jenna's behavior, but you don't want to say anything that might upset Jenna more. Instead, you say, "Can I ask Ellie some questions?"

"Sure," Jenna replies. "Go for it."

"Ellie, hi. I know there's a lot going on here today that you're probably not used to…. Um, I'm just thinking, you know, men can be jerks sometimes, and they don't always treat women well. They can be controlling and abusive. Were you trying to get revenge on someone for something they did to you?"

You pause, hoping that a voice will appear on your recorder with an answer.

"Who was your favorite person in life. Maybe your mother?" you ask and pause. "Did you have any brothers or sisters? Or a best friend?"

"Good questions," Jenna says quietly. "Keep going."

"Um… it's- it's hard, doing this… having a conversation. We think you can hear us, but we cannot hear you, so we're guessing. But we really want to know your story. We want to know all about you, Ellie. Can you tell us about your life?"

You pause, breathing low and slowly, afraid that your breath will cover up a disembodied voice.

"This is your chance, Ellie. What do you want the world to know about you?"

Pause. The silence hurts your ears.

And then, there is a loud bang and the floor below your feet shakes.

"What was that?" Jenna asks. She grabs for the walkie and presses the button. "Dave, was that you? Is everything okay?"

But there is no response on the walkie.

Jenna tries again. "Dave, are you okay?"

Again, there is no response.

"Josie, Simon – have you seen Dave?"

A crackle comes back and then Simon's voice says, "I thought he was with you."

"He was. Okay, back to the equipment room immediately," she says and charges for the door.

You barely keep up with her as she hurries back down the hall, through the large room, and down the stairs. When she reaches the first floor, she starts yelling, "Dave! Answer me now!"

She reaches the equipment room and turns on the light, causing you to lift a hand to shield your eyes, and you hear her say, "He's not here!"

Moments later, Josie and Simon come running down the hallway. "We need to search the place," he says.

"Yes, but we cannot split up! We stick together in pairs, got it?" Jenna commands. "And turn the lights on as you go. No more of this darkness!"

You all agree.

"We'll start in the basement," Simon says, and he and Josie start down the hall.

Jenna looks at you and says, "Let's check all these rooms together."

You just nod and follow her. You take turns flipping the light switches and looking into the rooms while never taking your eyes off each other. In between, Jenna is pleading with Dave on the walkie. "Dave, this isn't funny! Answer me!"

You encounter Simon and Josie, who both shake their heads indicating no sign of Dave, as you reach the stairs.

"You two take the second floor," Jenna says to them. "We'll go up to the third floor."

Up on the third floor, you do the same thing, turning on the lights and taking turns looking into each room, each closet, each crevice, while keeping an eye on each other. Jenna's pleading on the walkie becomes less frequent as her fear increases.

You are hurrying up to the fourth level when Josie and Simon come up behind you. Simon is on his walkie saying, "Dave, if you're fooling around, I will kill you!"

The four of you hurry through the rooms, checking each one, including the tower, with no signs of Dave.

"There's just this one room that won't open," Jenna says, going to the only closed door in the hall.

"He can't be in there," Simon says. "I've tried to get that door open a dozen times tonight and it won't budge."

"But, what if…?" Jenna pleads with her brother.

He just shrugs.

Jenna presses herself against the door and knocks. "Dave, are you in there? Dave, please answer me!"

She listens with her ear pressed to the crack where the door meets the jamb. "I think I hear movement inside!"

Simon rolls his eyes and says, "Okay, step back," and he takes a running leap at the door, throwing his entire body weight at the wooden surface, and you are surprised when you hear a thick scraping sound, then a pop, and Simon falls into the room.

"Yes!" Jenna exclaims and runs into the room. She flips the switch, and nothing happens, but light from the hallway is now pouring into the room, and aside from some old office furniture, the room is empty.

But Jenna, in true form, whips out a flashlight and checks every corner and under each piece of furniture. "You never know," she says, as though she hears silent judging from someone. She stands, straightens herself, and sighs.

"Maybe he's outside," you say, breaking the silence.

"Yes!" Jenna exclaims. "We haven't checked outside! He could be in the car, asleep!" she says.

You all follow in skeptical silence. You haven't known Dave long, but you know him enough to understand that he isn't the kind of person to wander off or hide from his friends. As this realization settles over you, dread takes over and your legs almost buckle underneath you as you follow your new friends back downstairs.

Jenna is practically running and is the first one outside. She checks Dave's car which is sitting empty, then the port-a-potty which is also empty.

In the light now pouring from the windows of the building, you see that Jenna's face is shiny, wet with tears. "I'm calling Mom and Dad," Jenna says, her voice choked.

"I'm calling 9-1-1," Simon says.

They both get on their cell phones and start talking. You turn away, confused and scared, and your gaze falls on Josie who is taking slow steps backward, her face drawn and pale, her eyes wide with fright.

"Josie?" you say. "Are you okay?"

She looks at you and shakes her head.

"You look like you're going to be sick," you say to her, approaching her. "Do you want to sit down or something?"

She keeps shaking her head, then says quietly, "I can't. I can't do this."

"Do what?" you ask. "Does it have something to do with Dave's disappearance?"

Suddenly, the area is flooded with headlights and flashing emergency lights as parents, police, and firefighters arrive, preventing you from getting an answer from Josie. She seems to melt into the background, skirting the crowd of people until you lose sight of her. You then decide that the best thing you can do is go to Jenna and try to help her through the chaos.

* * * * *

No sign of Dave is found that night. You and the rest of your friends are grilled by the police, and you each take a lie-detector test. Despite everyone passing the test, rumors start swirling that someone in the friend group killed Dave.

Jenna is never the same. When you see her in the halls at school, she gives you a wave, but her eyes are vacant, and her smile is forced. You don't see Josie again and rumors make their way through the school that she has been checked into a mental institution. About a month after that night, there is a fire in the old factory that, according to reports, destroys the top half of the building. A part of you wonders if it was one of your former friends who started the fire.

Twenty years pass, and then one day, you see a news story that the old mill property had finally been purchased and demolished. Workers then started to drain the swamp in an effort to fill it in and build on it, but they began to discover bodies preserved in the thick layer of muck at the bottom, one of which is identified through dental records as Dave Miller.

The news story also informs you that a memorial service is being held for Dave that afternoon in the auditorium at your old high school. You drop everything and rush out the door. You have just enough time to make it.

214

THE END

You follow behind Simon and Jenna as they head for the stairs. Jenna presses the button on the walkie. "Dave, are you and Josie done the walk through?"

Dave's voice comes back, "Josie says yes."

"Alright, head to the equipment room. We're going to regroup," she tells him.

"You got it, Babe," says Dave.

As you go down the stairs, you glance back over your shoulder, feeling like eyes are on you, and you remember that shadowed form that peeked into the room at you and Simon. A shiver runs up your back and you hurry on down the stairs.

But the feeling stays with you the whole way down the stairs, and your heartbeat starts pounding hard in your chest. You reach the first floor and continue following your friends down the hall, when you say, "Um, guys? I don't feel...." Everything goes black and stars pop before your eyes, then your body goes heavy, and you feel yourself falling to the ground.

All is dark and silent. "Am I dead?" you hear yourself ask, though you aren't sure your mouth moved.

"No, you are not dead," you hear. The voice is feminine and musical, like several clear notes of a fine crystal. Then you see a light getting brighter and brighter. Like the voice, the light is multifaceted, bright white but with threads of every other color in existence. A form emerges from the light, also feminine, draped in a robe made of the light.

"Who are you? Are you a ghost?"

"I am here to tell you, to assure you that you are safe. I am here to protect you from harm. You are safe," she says. Her face is beautiful like the light and her voice, though her mouth doesn't move.

"Do you have a name?" you ask.

"What do you want to call me?" she replies.

You look at her for a moment. "You are a myriad of colors. Can I call you Myriad?"

Her head bobs slightly. "Yes, you can call me Myriad."

"And you'll stay with me tonight?" you ask.

"I'll be with you for as long as you need me," she says.

Suddenly, your eyes pop open, and the lights of four people are shining in your face. You can feel the cold floor beneath your back.

"Can you guys get your lights out of my eyes?" you ask.

"Sorry!" Jenna, Dave, Simon, and Josie all say.

"How do you feel?" Simon asks, kneeling beside you.

"Fine. Better. Did I pass out?" you ask.

Simon chuckles. "Yes, you did. Scared us more than any ghost so far," he says.

"I think it was me scaring myself again that made me pass out," you say.

"Yes, that can happen," he says. "Alright, shall we try to get you up?"

You nod.

Dave and Simon reach out to help you stand. "Slowly, now," says Simon. When you are standing, he asks, "You okay?"

"Yes," you reply, feeling sturdy and strong, knowing that Myriad is with you even if you cannot see her now.

When you all reach the equipment room, everyone sits. Simon hands out bottles of water and Jenna pulls out a large plastic container.

"Chocolate chip cookies!" Dave exclaims. "Babe, you are the best," he says, reaching in and grabbing a few cookies.

"I know, but they *are* to share," she says, and passes the container to you. You take two cookies and pass it to Josie.

"Chocolate really is fortifying against ghosts," Josie says. "Like in *Harry Potter and the Prisoner of Azkaban*."

"That Lupin gives to Harry after he passes out on the train!" you say.

"Yes!" says Josie. "It's good to know we have another *Harry Potter* fan with us." She smiles at you, and you feel warmed by how your new friends are treating you.

"Alright, so now that we have water and cookies," Jenna starts, "Josie, do you want to give us a run-down of what – and who – you've encountered?"

Josie swallows her last bite of cookie and starts: "There's a *ton* of energy here. The toil of the workers and the demands of the management are soaked into every inch of this place. And there are a lot of ghosts. Some were so abused when they worked here that they hide in the shadows and won't even talk to me."

"But you talked to some?" Jenna asks, a hint of panic in her tone that you find a bit amusing.

"Yes, Jenna. I'll start from the top and work my way down," Josie says. "First, in the tower, is Corey, the homeless guy. It does seem like he accidentally OD'd, but I think he was being harassed by some of the ghosts and that kind of drove him to it. Like, normally, the drugs would drown out the voices in his head, but this time, the drugs didn't work because it wasn't voices in his head. But he didn't know that, so he took more and more until... you know. He's not very nice and tried to grope me."

"What?" Simon exclaims, standing suddenly and sending half a cookie sliding across the floor.

"It's okay, Simon. One of Dave's Guides restrained him," she says, and he sits again.

"Can I ask a question?" you interrupt.

"Of course," says Josie.

"What do you mean by 'one of Dave's Guides'?" you ask.

"Oh, I was referring to his Spirit Guide, a spirit that is with him to guide him in life. We all have them," she says.

"We do?"

"Yeah," Josie nods and smiles.

"Okay, no offense, but we can talk about Guides later. Let's get back to who we're dealing with here," Jenna says.

"Jenna! That's kind of rude!" Josie replies.

"No, it's fine," you say. You don't want to cause problems. "Jenna's right, we can talk about that later. I want to hear who you encountered here, too."

Josie lets out a huff of air and says, "Okay, so fourth floor… there's a man who I believe was the owner of this place when it was first built and operating. I think his office was up there, so he mostly stays up there. He shows himself as a tall, slender shadow-figure. He doesn't like that we are here. I sense that he is hiding some secrets."

You and Simon exchange knowing glances.

"Did you get a name?" Jenna asks.

"Jeffrey, I think. I didn't get a last name," Josie replies, then goes on. "On the third floor I encountered a spirit that had kind of been following us around most of the night but was finally able to draw him out. His name was Bobby, and he died at 9 years old when his arm got stuck in a piece of equipment. He's a bit of a mischief-maker, I think, so be careful. He runs all over this place and likes to play hide-and-seek. He seems to have befriended Sam, a man who was a manager here, I think, not at the same time as when Bobby died. He seems to try to keep an eye on things around here, though they avoid Jeffrey.

"On the second floor, in the breakroom, you'll find Ellie Watson, a black-widow-type woman who preyed on the lonely workers. She stole their money and their lives, from what I can tell. At least one of her victims is hanging around up there though I doubt many people experience him. His name is Martin.

"On this level I encountered a couple more workers, a father and son duo – Edward and Edward Junior who they called Eddie – who don't know they're dead. They still think they are here to do their jobs. I think they were the ones moving things around on the construction crew – although Bobby probably did some of it, too – but they weren't being mischievous, they just thought the stuff was in the way or put in the wrong place.

"Then, in the basement, is a nasty guy who I think angered the wrong person with his attitude and ended up murdered and his body was dumped out back in the swamp. He mostly hangs out in the basement area and tries to scare people as much as he can."

"That's it?" Jenna asks.

"Isn't that enough?" Josie asks. She takes another cookie and takes a bite. "We're only partly through the night and I'm exhausted."

"Sorry, I didn't mean it that way," Jenna says. "I meant, was there anything else you may have forgotten?"

Josie chuckles. "No, I covered everything I have encountered so far."

"Okay, well… that was pretty amazing, if you ask me. There is a lot here!" Jenna says, brightening. "I knew this place would be a paranormal gold mine!"

"So, what should we do next?" asks Dave.

If you investigate as a group, go to page 183
If you split up into two groups, go to page 201

"Okay, Simon and Josie, why don't you guys go up to the tower, and the three of us will go to the second-floor break room," Jenna says.

"Sounds like a plan," Josie says. She looks at Simon, and you see a little twinkle in her eyes. "Ready, Simon?"

"Let's go," he replies with a smile, but you sense a thread of nervous excitement in him, and they disappear into the dark hallway.

Jenna looks around at all the equipment, stuffs a few things into a backpack, and says, "I think I have everything. Let's go!"

A wave of excitement comes over you as you follow Jenna and Dave out into the dark hallway where Simon and Josie are no longer visible. You feel like you are finally really investigating.

The long, dark hallway and darkened doorways give you the feeling that you are being watched by things you cannot see, so you remain alert as you make your way to the stairs. At one point, you hear what sounds like footsteps behind you but when you spin around, no one is there.

You follow Jenna and Dave up the stairs and through the large, empty room. Jenna and Dave are talking quietly, and you can't quite hear what they're saying, as you are still listening for the sound of footsteps behind you to return.

At the other end of the large room, you all head down the short hallway and as you get closer, you can see the room with the debris all over the floor.

"Let me go first," Jenna says, and steps inside while Dave hovers in the doorway. You stand next to him, looking in and watching Jenna.

"Can I ask you something?" you say quietly to Dave.

"Sure," he replies.

"Josie and Simon… they, um, like… *like* each other, right?" you ask.

"Pfff, no!" Jenna scoffs. "Besides, he has a girlfriend."

"That doesn't always mean anything," Dave says, shaking his head. Then he looks at you and says, "You're very perceptive."

"Am I? I thought it was pretty obvious," you say.

Dave laughs and then you realize Jenna is scowling deeply at you. "You are both delusional if you think they like each other," she says.

"Babe, you know it's not that far-fetched," Dave says.

"She's my best friend and he's my brother," she says, as if that is all the answer you both need.

"Yeah, and I was Simon's best friend before I became *your* boyfriend," he replies. "So, what's the problem."

"There's no problem. It's just not a thing," she says matter-of-factly.

Just then, something goes flying across the room behind Jenna and the shattering of glass can be heard. She visibly jumps and spins around.

"What the—," she starts, but the shattering of another glass dish interrupts her. Then another dish goes flying and smashes.

"Babe, get out here," Dave says, but Jenna is standing in the middle of chaos with her camera going and a huge smile on her face. "Babe! You're going to get hurt!"

"I don't like this!" you say, terror rising within you for yourself and for your friend.

Finally, Dave says to you, "Stay here," and then dashes into the room, grabs Jenna in a bear hug, and drags her out of the room just as two more dishes go flying and smash against the wall.

"What did you do that for?" Jenna asks him after pushing free from his arms.

"You were going to get a plate to the skull if you didn't get out of there," he replies.

"I was fine!" she insists.

"Jenna, you were in danger. Glass dishes were flying across the room you were standing in, and you don't see a problem with that?" he says.

"No. I was getting amazing evidence!" she replies.

"Babe, I think you were being affected by the ghost or energy or whatever is in that room. That 'Black Widow' ghost Josie mentioned, combined with your disdain for the idea of Josie and Simon liking each other—"

"I don't dis—" Another plate smashes against the wall. Jenna steps back, puts her hands up like she is surrendering, closes her eyes, and takes a deep breath. Calmly and softly, she says, "Okay, maybe I do have some *slight concerns* with what you are talking about, but now is not the time or place for such discussions. Alright?"

Your face burns with embarrassment. "I'm sorry, Jenna. I didn't know," you say.

"No, it's okay, really. You had no way of knowing that would push a button," she laughs and shakes her head. "But wow, what a crazy experience that was! And thanks for saving me, Babe," she says to Dave and gives him a kiss.

"You're not going back in there, are you?" he asks.

"Well, yeah. I think it will be okay. I've calmed down. And I want to investigate. I think we should do an EVP session in here," she replies.

Dave shakes his head but agrees, "Okay, if that's what you want."

Cautiously, Jenna steps back over the threshold into the room and pauses. You can see she is tense, waiting for another dish to smash. She shines her flashlight at the cabinets on the far wall, and visibly relaxes. "I think we're in luck. Doesn't look like there are any dishes left for this lady to throw."

You chuckle nervously and step into the room with Jenna.

Behind you, Dave says, "I'll stay here and stand guard, if that's okay."

"Sure, Babe," Jenna replies. She moves into the center of the room and says, "Ellie, are you still here with us? That was a pretty impressive display of power you showed us, but now we would like to talk to you."

She pauses.

"Ellie, we've heard that some people call you a 'Black Widow'…. How do you feel about that?"

Another pause.

You have an eerie sensation that something is happening, though you cannot see or hear anything at the moment. "Does the air feel charged to you?" you ask.

"Yes!" Jenna replies. "Like static electricity! Dave, seriously, come inside just for a minute and see if you can feel it too."

Dave sighs and steps forward into the room slowly. He takes another step, and another, towards Jenna, his hands out, as if feeling his way along.

"Well?" Jenna prompts.

"Well… I… I think… I don't know…," he frowns and then jumps forward and turns to look behind him. "Whoa!"

"What happened?" Jenna asked.

"I think she just grabbed my butt!" he says.

You look at Jenna and she looks at you, and you both burst out laughing.

"It's not funny!" Dave says. "That's assault!"

Jenna, still laughing, replies, "I don't think someone nicknamed 'Black Widow' cares if she's got permission or not."

"She has a point," you say, your laughter abating.

"She likes you!" Jenna says. "Now you have to stay, or we may not get anything else from her."

"I'm not sure I like being used as bait, Jenna," Dave says.

Her face falls. "You're not serious," she says and chuckles, but it lacks confidence.

"I am serious, Jenna. I've been the unwitting puppet of a ghost before, and I did not like it. I don't want to put myself in that position again," he says.

Your jaw drops at this statement as you look to Jenna for her response.

She takes a step back. "Okay. You're right. It's not fair for me to assume you'll put yourself in a situation that may be risky. I'm sorry," she says.

"Thank you," he replies.

"Alright. So, do you want to leave and go back to the equipment room? Or stay just outside the room?" she asks him.

He looks at you. "What do you think?"

If he should stay outside the room, go to page 198
If he should go to the equipment room, go to page 208

Seemingly all at once, everyone charges from the room after Josie. You can hear her yelling "No, no, no, no, no, no, no!" continuously as she runs down the stairs. Though you have only known Josie a short time, you know her enough to know that this is not normal behavior. Something bad, something serious, has happened.

Several times you stumble as you run down the stairs, later swearing that each time it felt like someone tried to trip you, but each time you are able to catch yourself.

On the first floor, you all follow the trail of Josie back down the hallway, through the equipment room, and outside. You all find Josie sitting on the curb at the far end of the parking lot under the only streetlight in the vicinity that works. She has her head in her hands and is muttering, "No, no, no, no, no! I can't, I can't, I can't, I can't, I can't, I can't, I can't. No, no, no, no, no! I can't, I can't, I can't, I can't!"

Simon reaches her first, sits down next to her, puts his arms around her, and pulls her close. "Josie, it's okay. You're okay. You're out of there."

She lifts her head and looks at him but continues with her ramblings. ""No, no, no, no, no! I can't, I can't, I can't. It's too much. It's too much. It's too much."

"What happened?" Jenna asks Josie, but she is unable to answer.

"Babe, I think we need to call it," Dave says.

Jenna groans, but says, "I know you're right but…."

"Your best friend is falling apart, Jenna!" Simon says. "We're done! I'm calling her an ambulance!" He pulls his cell from his pocket and dials.

"Babe, I'm going to grab everything from the equipment room and lock up. We can come back and get the rest tomorrow," Dave says to Jenna.

"Okay, fine," she says, groaning again.

Simon is again holding Josie who has stopped muttering but is crying into his shirt. "I hate this place," he says, staring up at the building.

You turn and look at the towering structure, and in each of the windows you see shadowed forms staring back at you, and you swear you can feel their sense of victory.

THE END

Something about the whispers in the shadows frightens you, so you head toward the light, hoping it is your friends. Maybe they decided to pack things up while you were unconscious, so you could all leave once you woke. You can't wait to leave this place, so you hurry down the hall toward the light. It seems longer than you remember. You start to run, anxious to leave. The light is growing bigger before you as you hurry. And then the fear starts to melt from you. You can see movement within the lighted doorway and feel love and peace coming from whoever is inside. You are no longer certain it is your friends, but you are no longer afraid. You rush into the lighted doorway, cross the threshold, and feel your entire being expand in the most wonderful way, as though you are surrounded by only the purest form of love. It is warm, comfortable, peaceful, and joyful. It feels like everything that is good and right. You feel yourself being lifted up, up, up into it until....

THE END

You reach the basement, and everyone is waiting for you, standing around the salt circle Josie placed earlier.

"Okay, you can keep recording but I need you to put the cameras down, form a circle on the outside of the salt circle, and hold hands," Josie says.

You look to Jenna for guidance and then place the camera on the floor facing Josie. You then take your place around the circle. You have Simon on one side of you and Jenna on the other. Everyone joins hands.

"I need everyone to project energy of unconditional love into the circle," Josie says, taking Simon's other hand and holding Dave's hand on her other side. "Do you all understand what I mean when I say that?"

No one says anything, so Josie continues. "Come on, guys, it means that you have to project love to the souls trapped here no matter who they are or what they did in life. That even if they were a really bad person when they were alive, we will show them love."

"You can't be serious," Simon scoffs.

"Ugh," Josie groans and rolls her eyes. She releases Dave's hand and turns Simon towards her. "Yes, I am serious, Simon. You have to put aside your judgements of these souls. You of all people, being *Empathic*, should be able to understand that even people who do bad things are hurting and are desperately in need of love. You have to trust me on this."

"O-okay," he stutters in response.

"You'll at least try?" she asks.

"Yes," he replies.

Josie takes her place in the circle once again. "That's all I ask, is that you all try to do this to the best of your ability. Okay, so, please everyone, focus your energy into the circle...." She closes her eyes and tilts her head back a little. You can tell she is doing something, but you don't know what. You want to say something, but then Jenna speaks.

"Josie, I know you need to focus, but if you can describe what you're experiencing – for the recorders – that would be great," she says softly.

"I will," Josie replies. "Just focus, please." She takes a deep breath and continues. "I want you all to feel the feeling of unconditional love within yourself, and then I want you to send that feeling out through your heart into the circle before us. You can imagine it as a beam of beautiful colored light, you can imagine it as a ball of energy, or like a flow of water. Whatever works for you, just send that into the circle."

Josie then closes her eyes, raises her chin, and speaks into the air, "This circle before us represents the heart of this land and this structure, and this heart is hurt, angry, and sick. We offer our unconditional love to the heart of this place in hopes of healing, of repairing all the damage that has been done. We send love and healing into the circle and apologize for the war that took place upon this land, where both sides were doing what they thought was right for their people, where neither side won, and both sides lost. Mistakes were made by all, but all mistakes can be forgiven. We ask now for the heart of this land to forgive and accept our unconditional love."

At first you feel silly trying to do what Josie has asked, but then, as she talks, you start to feel something happening. There is a warmth growing in your chest that makes you feel good, and your hands tingle like when you put your hands on the plasma ball at the Museum of Science. When you look at your own hands and those of your friends in the circle, you swear you can see tiny sparkling lights, similar to what you saw earlier passing between Josie and Simon.

Josie continues. "We send love and healing into the circle and apologize for the building of this structure, for the cruel way the earth was dug out, for the misguided intentions and greed of some of those who built this place, who acted with only their own gain in mind. Mistakes were made by all, but all mistakes can be forgiven. We ask now for the heart of this land to forgive and accept our unconditional love."

Now you feel a sort of rumbling under your feet, as though an engine is running within the ground. "Keep focusing, you guys!" Josie says and then goes on, speaking louder. "We send love and healing into the circle and apologize for the misguided person who used the pain, anger, and sickness from the land to manipulate dark energy, to bring forth more pain and suffering into the world. We send love and healing into the circle and apologize for those who knowingly and unknowingly did bad things with that energy. Mistakes were made by all, but all mistakes can be forgiven. We ask now for the heart of this land to forgive and accept our unconditional love."

More rumbling comes, more tingles in your hands, and you feel a bigger tug at your heart.

"I now call on the spirit guides and loved ones of all of us present and of all who have lost their lives on this land and in this building…."

Now you can see the sparkles of light leaving your hands and the hands of your friends as it floats toward the circle and starts to swirl in a slow-motion tornado-like movement. It continues to strengthen as Josie goes on.

"I call on the spirits of this land to join us and help repair this deep wound. Help the land remember what it was like before anyone came to make trouble, before digging, before war. Help us help the land remember what it is like to be good, to be whole, to be healthy."

The vibration under your feet seems to change, almost like it is softening.

"I call on the spirits of all the innocent people who lost their lives here, to offer their forgiveness to the land and forgiveness to the souls that did harm to them…."

The vibration intensifies again, and you feel a surge of energy from within your chest. A burst of sparkling energy rushes from everyone's clasped hands and floats into the whirlpool swirling before you, and you realize then that you have tears running down your cheeks. You glance quickly at your friends and realize that in the soft light of the energy, you can see that they, too, all have wet cheeks.

Josie continues her monologue, her voice increasing in intensity. "Mistakes were made by all, but all mistakes can be forgiven. Mistakes were made by all, but all mistakes can be forgiven. Mistakes were made by all, but all mistakes can be forgiven. We ask now for the heart of this land to forgive and accept our unconditional love. We ask now for all the bad to be turned to good, for all fear to become opportunity, for all hate to become love, for all death to become rebirth!"

Then, a shockwave blasts from within the salt circle. You are all thrown backwards, landing flat on your backs, and you all lose consciousness.

When you each come to with groans and grunts, Josie declares, "It's done! We fixed it! And everyone has moved on!"

* * * * *

Later, as everyone is packing up the equipment, Josie tells you all how when you felt only a slight vibration and saw small sparks of energy, she felt an earthquake and saw a storm of energy moving with a mighty force within the salt circle. She tells you of watching each of the souls move on through that maelstrom, from the innocent ones who went happily and gratefully to the more resistant souls like Sam, Edward, Bobby, and Ellie the Black Widow. The most challenging soul to move on was Jeffrey, the original owner of the building.

"If there was a bad thing to be done to someone, he did it," Josie tells you all. "From cheating his employees to paying a nurse to kill the newborn babies of his mistresses."

"What the heck!" Jenna exclaims, her face twisting in disgust.

"I know, right?" Josie nods. "Well, some beings came through and kind of *dragged* him into the vortex, kicking and screaming. It was almost funny to witness."

"What do you mean by 'beings'?" you ask.

Josie shrugs. "Can't say, really. They were just light forms, but they felt very intense."

"Wow," you breathe.

"Okay, I think everything is packed up," Jenna says. "Are we good to go?"

Everyone nods.

As you all walk out into the night and Dave locks the door behind you, Jenna says, "This place sure seems different now, doesn't it?"

Again, everyone nods.

* * * * *

Over the course of the next two weeks, you and the others gather at Jenna's house to review evidence in between doing homework. Jenna becomes extremely excited as the amount of evidence continues to pile up from the investigation, from extremely clear EVPs to shadows moving on camera to objects being thrown. Free-floating balls of light are seen on screen, and conversations are heard on recorders in rooms when none of the living people were in there.

You are impressed by the level of detail Jenna goes to in order to confirm evidence, lining up different recordings from audio and video to prove someone was or was not present when various activity was happening.

The following Friday you are accosted by Jenna in the hallway at school as you are heading to the cafeteria for lunch. Her curly, carrot-colored hair is more disheveled than usual, and her face is red, but her eyes are shining, and she is smiling bigger than you have seen before. "Come! Now!" she says as she takes you by the arm and drags you down the hall. She leads you into a classroom that is empty except for Dave, Josie, and Simon, who apparently have also been summoned to the impromptu meeting by Jenna.

"You guys are never going to believe this!" Jenna starts, breathless.

"What is it?" Josie asks.

"I submitted evidence clips and a written report of our investigation to a parapsychologist named Paul Adenbonne out of Rhode Island and he wants to meet with us this weekend!" Jenna looks at you all expectantly, but the news doesn't seem to hit the rest of you the way it does to Jenna.

Her face falls. "Guys, this is a big deal! He's famous in the paranormal community, and he thinks we have real evidence!"

"That's great, Jenna!" you say.

"What do you need from us?" Simon asks.

"Just be willing to meet with him and tell him your experiences," Jenna replies. "Can you guys do that?"

"Of course, Babe," Dave answers first.

"Yes, sure," both Simon and Josie say.

"I'm in," you reply.

"Great! Guys, we're going to be famous!" Jenna exclaims, clapping her hands.

Everyone chuckles.

THE END

www.ingramcontent.com/pod-product-compliance
Lightning Source LLC
Chambersburg PA
CBHW070639100726
47907CB00007B/2037